A PERFECT MANHATTAN MURDER

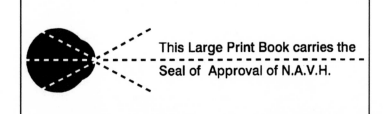

This Large Print Book carries the
Seal of Approval of N.A.V.H.

A NIC & NIGEL MYSTERY

A PERFECT MANHATTAN MURDER

TRACY KIELY

THORNDIKE PRESS
A part of Gale, a Cengage Company

Farmington Hills, Mich • San Francisco • New York • Waterville, Maine
Meriden, Conn • Mason, Ohio • Chicago

LIBRARY OF CONGRESS CATALOGING-IN-PUBLICATION DATA

Names: Kiely, Tracy, author.
Title: A perfect Manhattan murder / by Tracy Kiely.
Description: Large print edition. | Waterville, Maine : Thorndike Press, a part of Gale, Cengage Learning, 2017. | Series: Thorndike Press large print mystery | Series: A Nic & Nigel mystery
Identifiers: LCCN 2017018889| ISBN 9781432842277 (hardcover) | ISBN 1432842277 (hardcover)
Subjects: LCSH: Murder—Investigation—Fiction. | Large type books. | GSAFD: Mystery fiction.
Classification: LCC PS3611.I4453 P47 2017b | DDC 813/.6—dc23
LC record available at https://lccn.loc.gov/2017018889

Published in 2017 by arrangement with Midnight, Ink, an imprint of Llewellyn Publications, Woodbury, MN 55125-2989

Printed in the United States of America
1 2 3 4 5 6 7 21 20 19 18 17

Once again, to Matt.

ACKNOWLEDGMENTS

Once again, I have many people I need to thank: Barbara Poelle, who is not only an amazing agent, but one of the funniest people I know; Terri Bischoff, my very patient editor, who along with keeping me on track, stoically puts up with Linda Joffe Hull and my truly terrible ideas for cat-themed mystery titles, and Aimee Hix and me in general; Dan Brown, who kindly explained to me that not all scotch is created equal; Barbara Kiely, my international rebel of a mother-in-law, who always reads my drafts; Matt Kiely, my always amazing husband; and Jack, Elizabeth, and Pat, three of the greatest kids any parent could ask for. Thank you all!

ONE

"Nigel, darling," I said as I readjusted the beaded strap of my bias cut gown, "if you poke me with that thing one more time, I'm going to beat you over the head with it."

Nigel arched a black brow and regarded the item in question. "That would certainly give housekeeping something to talk about," he conceded as he twirled the gold-tipped cane in his hand.

"I believe Skippy already accomplished that," I replied with a pointed nod at the giant Bullmastiff currently sprawled across our bed. At the sound of his name, Skippy opened one sleepy brown eye and gazed at me a moment before closing it again. "Speaking of which," I continued, "remind me to send flowers to that poor girl from room service this morning. What on earth made you order bacon, anyway?" I asked as I tugged a silk white glove up and over my elbow. "You know what the smell does to him."

"A momentary lapse of judgment," Nigel agreed absentmindedly, his attention on tossing and tapping the cane.

I watched in silence as he nearly took out the desk lamp. "Don't you think that it's time to retire that thing?" I finally asked.

"You heard the doctor. I busted my ankle."

I crossed my arms and stared at him a beat. "You *sprained* your ankle," I reminded him. "Three weeks ago."

Nigel waved his hand at me. "You say potato, I say . . ."

"Poser?" I offered.

Nigel laughed. "Me? A poser?"

"Yes, you. Ever since that nurse told you the cane made you look dashing, it's become a third appendage."

Nigel pulled his brows together as if trying to place who I meant. "What nurse?" he finally asked.

"You know. The blonde."

Nigel stared at me vacantly.

I sighed. Spreading out my hands, I cupped them in front of my chest to pantomime her other memorable feature. "She also had really . . ."

Nigel frowned. "Bad arthritis?"

I rolled my eyes. "Cleavage, Nigel. Cleavage."

10

His face cleared. "Ah, yes. I remember her." He paused. "Wait. She was a blonde?"

I smiled sweetly as I picked up an empty water glass and threw it at his head. Nigel let out a bark of laughter as he neatly caught it. "Now, darling," he said, as he crossed to me, "as much as I love it when you get jealous, you know I only have eyes for you."

I turned my back to him and picked up my lipstick tube from the dressing table. As I uncapped it, Nigel leaned down and kissed my neck. Lightly tracing his fingers down my exposed back, he added, "I like your dress."

"I thought you might," I said as I applied more color to my lips. "Consider it my atonement for accepting Harper's invitation to dinner."

Harper and I went to school together. Nigel and I were in town to attend the opening night of a new Broadway show written by another schoolmate of ours, Peggy McGrath. When Harper had called to suggest that we join her and her husband, Dan, for dinner before the show, I assumed that it wouldn't just be the four of us. I assumed wrong. I had forgotten that most of our college friends found Dan just as odious as I did.

Nigel didn't respond. Instead he kissed

my neck again. I peeked over my shoulder at him. "Does this mean I'm forgiven?" I asked.

Nigel shook his head. "Nope. You're still in the penalty box. However, I have it on good authority that the ref is not averse to bribes."

"Oh, really?" I turned around and leaned in close. Lowering my voice to a conspiratorial whisper, I asked, "What's his weakness?"

"Martinis and lanky redheads with wicked jaws."

"As long as you reverse the order, we may be able to come to some sort of an agreement," I told him.

"Oh?"

There was a polite knock on our door. I stood on my tiptoes and lightly kissed his mouth. "I called down to room service for a pitcher of martinis while you were in the shower."

"You're a wily woman, Mrs. Martini."

"I know, dear. Now, put some pants on while I answer the door."

Two

Most hotels provide various family care services, and the Ritz is no exception. However, based on the startled look on the fresh-faced young woman who now stood uncertainly in our sitting area, I gathered that Nigel had not made it clear that the "little guy" who needed a sitter for the night was canine and not human.

"I was told that you needed a babysitter for a three-year-old boy," said the woman, who had only moments ago cheerfully introduced herself as Maureen, adding that she "just loved kids." Skippy had bounded off the bed at her entrance and now sat politely before her, his paw raised for her to shake.

"That we do," Nigel agreed cheerfully as if there was no confusion. "Skippy here is a good boy, for the most part, but like most three-year-olds, he needs supervision."

Maureen regarded Skippy warily. Skippy

13

stared back, his large fawn-colored head coming nearly to her waist. Shifting the pile of coloring books and crayons to her left arm, she gingerly shook Skippy's paw with her right. Skippy barked happily.

"We might be late," I said apologetically. "Please feel free to order anything you'd like from room service."

"I highly recommend the martinis," Nigel added as he fetched my coat. "Just don't let Skippy have more than one. They tend to put him in an amorous mood."

"That's you, dear," I corrected.

Nigel paused. "Right you are," he agreed after a moment. "Still," he added, turning to Maureen, "just to be on the safe side, I'd limit him to one."

THREE

Outside, there was a hint of fall in the cool, crisp September air. Given that the restaurant was a scant mile away, Nigel suggested that we walk. Given that I was wearing four-inch heels, I suggested he think again. Nigel saw my point. We took a cab.

Aureole's is located in the Bank of America Tower on 42nd Street. We entered to find the bistro-like lounge mobbed with pre-theater attendees. I spotted Harper and Dan almost immediately. It wasn't hard. At the large, perpetually boisterous bar they were conspicuous in their isolation. Dan didn't appear to mind the snubs, but I knew Harper did.

"There's Harper and Dan," I said jerking my chin in their direction.

Nigel glanced over. "I see that I am not alone in my estimation of Dan's social graces. Poor Harper."

"Well, you know what they say. You can't

marry the devil and not expect to get burned."

Nigel looked down at me. "Who ever said that?"

"My grandmother," I replied.

"Oh," he said after a moment. "Pithy."

"I thought so."

"Before we go over," Nigel said, "I think we should agree on a safe word."

"A safe word?"

"Yes, you know. A special word that lets the other know we need to leave."

I stopped and stared up at him. "Why do you think you might need to leave?"

"Dan."

"Dan," I repeated.

"Yes. He makes me want to punch him in the face. Repeatedly."

"That would be awkward," I agreed.

"Exactly. Which is why we should have a safe word."

I tried to suppress a smile and failed. "Fine. What's your safe word?"

"I was thinking of 'We-need-to-leave-right-now-or-I'm-going-to-punch-Dan-in-the-face.' "

"You forgot 'repeatedly.' "

"I won't when it counts."

I laughed as I grabbed his hand and began to pull him toward Harper. "First off," I said, "that's a sentence, and second, I think they might be able to crack the code."

Nigel reluctantly followed me to the backlit bar. "Fine," he grumbled before muttering something about *schadenfreude*. I ignored him and focused on Harper.

Harper had been my first real friend on campus freshman year, despite the fact that on the surface we had very little in common. She came from a prominent, moneyed family who expected nothing but the best from their only daughter. I came from a blue-collar family who couldn't understand why I wanted "some fancy pants education." Harper took me under her wing and taught me about wines, opera, and the difference between Monet and Manet. In return, I introduced her to boilermakers, *The Rocky Horror Picture Show,* and the difference between Ramen Noodles and Cup Noodles. It was a mutually beneficial alliance.

After graduation, Harper moved back to New York and took a job at *Vanity Fair* as a society columnist. It was an easy fit for her as she was mainly reporting on the lives of her family and friends. It was also there that she met Dan Trados, a young staff writer known for his fierce ambition — both social and professional — and caustic wit. After a whirlwind courtship, they were married. Within a year, Dan was running the drama desk and directing his barbs at Broadway. Within two years, he had earned himself the nickname The Bastard of Broadway. Within five years, the moniker had been shortened by half.

I hadn't seen much of Harper over the last few years, mainly because Nigel and I moved to LA. But even before that, our get-togethers had become infrequent at best. My career as a detective for the NYPD was about as far away as one could get from the glittering world in which Harper moved. The fact that Dan didn't exactly encourage our friendship hadn't helped either. Dan preferred to surround himself with the artistic and literary elite, and a detective from a working-class family simply did not fit into his preferred social circle. I couldn't fault him for this. A pompous narcissist didn't fit in with my social circle, either.

"Harper!" I said now, pulling her into a tight hug. "It's so good to see you!" She returned the hug, holding it a little longer than normal. With her wavy dark blond hair, perennial dewy skin, and lithe build, Harper is one of those women blessed with a kind of effortless beauty. I'd seen her roll out of bed after three hours of sleep looking better than most women did after a day of pampering at a spa. However, when she finally pulled back from the hug, I noticed faint purple shadows under her normally bright hazel eyes.

"You've no idea how glad I am to see you," she said simply. She was wearing an off-the-shoulder gown. The silk bodice was a bright salmon; the gauzy full skirt was a swirl of teal, coral, and green. It was a different look for Harper, who usually gravitated to more conservative colors, and I wondered if the gown wasn't intended to detract from her apparent fatigue.

"It has been too long," I agreed as Nigel leaned down to hug Harper as well. We then both turned and exchanged a far less enthusiastic greeting with Dan.

I'd once described Dan as a police sketch artist's nightmare, as he was a collection of unremarkable features. A little under six feet, he had a slim build that was the result of a high metabolism rather than any exercise routine. Nigel said he looked like a consumptive on the mend. His dark brown hair was neither thinning nor receding, his light brown eyes were framed with an appropriate number of lashes, and his mouth was neither wide nor thin. Perhaps to offset this blandness, he'd recently grown a beard.

The wispy salt-and-pepper Van Dyke certainly made an impression; however, probably not in the way he'd hoped.

On the plus side, he was intelligent, could be charming when he wanted, and (according to Nigel) had excellent taste in scotch. Actually, Nigel would rank those traits in reverse order.

I turned my attention back to Harper. "How's Gracie?" I asked.

Harper's round face lit up at the mention of her little girl. "She's amazing. She just turned six months. She's so perfect that I don't even mind that I can't seem to lose the baby weight." She paused, lightly patting her new curvier frame, and added ruefully, "Well, *most* of the time, anyway."

I lightly smacked her arm. "Don't be silly, you look as gorgeous as ever," I said. "I can't wait to see her."

Nigel seconded my opinion before turning to Dan and asking, "So how are you enjoying it?"

Dan, who had been eyeing the shapely backside of a passing waitress, blinked at Nigel in confusion. "Enjoying what?" he asked.

"Fatherhood," Nigel replied with deliberate patience.

"Oh, right," Dan idly stroked his chin as

he considered the question. "It's been fine," he finally said, "for the most part. I mean, obviously, there have been some changes." His eyes unconsciously drifted to Harper's hips. "But we're adjusting. I did end up renting an apartment near the Theater District to use as an office on the weekends. I don't know if Harper told you, but I've been asked to put together a kind of anthology of my best reviews along with some of my personal experiences and insider knowledge." He paused for us to congratulate him. We didn't. "Anyway, it was quite an unexpected honor and, of course, this is the time of year when the Broadway machine cranks up again. So far it's looking like it will be a busy season. And as I'm sure you can imagine, it's hard to write with a crying baby in the next room."

I stared at Dan for a beat while Harper busied herself with the catch on her pearl bracelet. "You stay in an apartment every weekend?" I finally asked.

Dan nodded absently. "It's really more of a grubby weekend office, but I find it's much more conducive to my way of working."

"How very nice for you, then," I said.

Harper knew me too well to miss the edge that had crept into my voice. She quickly

21

raised her eyes to mine; in them was a silent plea not to comment. With effort, I bit back my retort. Harper let out a small breath of relief. Pasting a bright smile on her face she said, "Enough about us. I want to hear all about that Hollywood scandal you two dug up. I thought you'd retired from the force, Nic."

"So had I," I admitted with a sigh.

"Well, go on then," Harper pressed eagerly. "Tell me all the juicy parts that the papers left out."

"There's not much else to tell, really," I said.

"Nic's just being modest," Nigel said, wrapping his arm around my shoulder. "She was brilliant. The police never would have solved it if it weren't for her."

"That's not true," I said. "Nigel did just as much, if not more, than I did. He's the one who ended up . . ."

". . . taking a bullet for Nic," Nigel finished with a spectacularly failed attempt at modesty.

Harper looked expectantly at Nigel, her eyes aglow with interest. "I heard. Now, I want to hear every detail," she instructed.

Nigel shrugged. "It's not something I like to make a big deal about."

"Says the man who gave six interviews

and was the cover story for *People*," I said laughing.

Harper smiled broadly. "Oh! I loved that article. Wait, how did they describe you again?" She closed her eyes in concentration. " 'Nigel Martini is the Cary Grant of our generation — charming, witty, and just a little bit dangerous,' " she quoted.

I laughed. "God, I wish I had a photographic memory like yours," I said. "College would have been so much easier."

"Wait, you were shot?" Dan suddenly asked. "Is that why you're using a cane?"

Nigel glanced down at his leg. "No, that's from something entirely different," he said. Ducking his head in embarrassment, he whispered, "I forgot the safe word. *Again.*"

"Nigel! Would you stop saying that?" I yelled as I slapped him upside the back of his head.

Harper let out a snort of laughter. Dan's eyes widened in shock. Turning to Harper, he asked, "Why didn't I know about this?"

"Their safe word?" Harper asked, her eyes bright with laughter.

Dan frowned at her. "No. About the shooting."

"I'm sure I told you about it," she said.

"It was in the tabloids," I said with false innocence.

"Actually, it was a little higher," Nigel confided to Dan before winking and adding, "Thank God."

Dan's nose twitched as if suddenly assailed by an unpleasant odor. "I don't read the tabloids," he said.

I turned to Dan, hoping to keep my face straight. "No? Well, then I'll be sure to get you a subscription for your birthday this year."

Harper pressed her lips together in an attempt not to laugh. Dan ignored my offer. "How is it that someone shot at you? When did this happen?" he asked instead.

"A few months back," I answered. "We sort of got involved in a murder case."

"And I took a bullet for Nic," Nigel repeated with a grin.

"You said that already," I reminded him.

"It was quite painful," he added.

"If I remember correctly," I murmured, "you said my nurse's uniform made up for it."

A small smile tugged at Nigel's lips. "True. Which is why I'd do it again."

"Well, I think it's the most romantic thing I've ever heard," Harper said with a laugh. Slipping her arm through Dan's, she teasingly asked, "What do you think, Dan? Would you take a bullet for me?"

"Given my last two reviews, I think the more likely scenario would be you having to take a bullet for *me,*" he replied as if it were a source of pride. "In which case, perhaps that baby fat might come in handy after all," he added with a hearty laugh. Seeing Harper's stricken expression, Dan flung his arm around her shoulders. "Oh, come on," he chided, giving her a quick side squeeze. "Don't be so sensitive. You know I'm your biggest fan."

"Well, you're certainly the biggest *something,*" Nigel muttered under his breath. Harper produced a thin smile but said nothing.

Dan registered neither reaction; his eyes were fixed on something or someone behind me. Dropping his arm from Harper's shoulders, he abruptly squared his own and said, "If you'll excuse me a moment, darling, there's someone I need to talk to."

We watched in silence as he disappeared into the crowd. When he was finally out of view, Harper closed her eyes and shook her head. "Don't say it, Nic. I already know," she said with a sigh.

"I wasn't going to say a word," I answered truthfully.

"Maybe," she responded. "But you were thinking it."

"Thinking what?" I asked.

Harper stared at me with sad eyes. "You're thinking that I'm married to the most self-absorbed man on the East Coast."

I opened my mouth to form some kind of protest, but Harper continued first, "But you're wrong," she said with a shake of her head.

"I didn't —" I began, but Harper interrupted me.

"You're wrong," she repeated firmly. "I'm not married to the most self-absorbed man on the East Coast. I'm married to the most self-absorbed man on the *planet.*" Signaling the bartender, she then asked, "Now, who wants a drink?"

FOUR

Once our drinks were firmly in hand, I turned to Harper. "So what happened?" I asked. "I thought you were happy."

Harper took a long sip of her gin and tonic before answering. "Gracie happened," she said. "Dan always told me that he wanted to have children, but when I got pregnant, he behaved as if it was nothing more than a silly hobby of mine. He didn't come to any of the doctor's appointments, and he wouldn't come with me to pick out furniture for the nursery. The night I went into labor, Dan was at the theater reviewing a new show. I texted him and told him to meet me at the hospital."

I felt my eyes go wide. "Please do not tell me that he didn't go to the hospital," I said.

Harper shook her head. "Oh no, he came all right. But it was four hours *later.* Not only did he stay for the entire play, but he went to the office to write up his notes while they were, and I quote, 'still fresh in his head.' "

"Oh Harper," I said, giving her arm a sympathetic squeeze, "I'm so sorry. I had no idea."

Harper shrugged. "I hardly see him anymore. He's always working on that damn book of his. I *think*. But it's fine. In a way, it's a good thing. I mean, the scales finally fell from my eyes, and I realized what a colossal jackass he is."

"Don't feel you need to mince words on my behalf," said Nigel. "Marriage to Nic has cured me of my delicate sensibilities."

I let out an inelegant snort. "You wouldn't know a delicate sensibility if it snuck up and bit you on the ass."

"That right there shows how little you know about delicate sensibilities," Nigel replied waving a scolding finger at me. "They wouldn't dream of doing something so crass."

I swatted his finger before turning back to Harper. "Have you told Dan how you feel?" I asked.

Harper let out a mirthless little laugh. "Are you kidding? Even if I did, he wouldn't believe me. His ego has grown to such proportions that I think I could walk up to him, tell him I hated him, *shoot* him, and he'd still think it was a misunderstanding."

"So what are you going to do?" I asked.

Harper took a deep breath. "Honestly? I don't know. I mean, I have to think about Gracie." She paused and added, "Even though *he* certainly doesn't." She took a sip of her drink. "I just know I can't continue with the way things are anymore."

"Meaning divorce?" I asked.

"I don't know," Harper sighed. "I don't want to make any rash decisions now, especially when I haven't slept through the night in months. And if I do decide to leave him, I'm going to need a damn good game plan."

"What do you mean?" I asked.

Harper glanced around and lowered her voice. "You've heard of a premarital contract, right?"

"Of course."

Harper sighed. "Well, in my stupid naivety, I thought that I didn't need one. Daddy pushed and pushed for me to get Dan to sign one, but I thought the very idea was disgusting. So I refused. The bottom line is that if I divorce Dan now, he gets half of everything."

I did not come from a family of wealth. I did, however, marry into one. The net worth of the Martini family is one of those figures that would cause your fingers to cramp if you were to write it out in longhand. However, compared to Harper's, they're barely scraping by. Even half of what little Harper controlled would still be a fortune.

"Harper," I began.

Harper raised her hand to stop me, saying, "Don't say it. I'm already kicking myself on a daily basis for that decision. But don't worry about me. I'll figure something out. And in the meantime, I'm focusing on two things: Gracie and not bashing in his face." She drained the rest of her drink. "Would anyone else care for another one?" she asked indicating her empty glass.

Nigel glanced down at his unfinished drink and shrugged. "Well, when in Rome, I always say," he replied as he tossed back the remains.

"We're not in Rome," I pointed out.

"Yes, but I have it on good authority that all roads lead there," he replied.

I considered his point. "Can't argue with that logic," I finally agreed as I did the same.

FIVE

Dan rejoined us several minutes later. His face was flushed and his mouth was pinched in annoyance. "Is everything all right?" Harper asked, laying her hand on his arm. "You look upset."

Dan shook his head, as well as his arm from her hand. "I'm fine," he said, his voice curt.

Harper gamely placed her hand back on his forearm and gave it a gentle pat. "Well, why don't I get you a drink then," she said soothingly.

Before anyone could protest her offer to leave the three of us alone, she was gone. Dan ignored us completely, silently staring at some unseen spot on the floor. Nigel gave me a pointed look and mouthed *safe word.* After several seconds of awkward silence, I asked, "So are you writing the review for Peggy's play?"

Dan glanced up blinking as if surprised to

find me there. "What?" he said.

I repeated the question. "Yes, of course, I'm reviewing it," he said with a sigh of irritation. "Why wouldn't I?"

I forced a polite smile. "Well, I just wondered if there might be a conflict of interest, as Peggy is one of Harper's best friends."

Dan snorted. "I think you just answered your question," he said. "Peggy is one of *Harper's* best friends. Not mine. Ergo, no conflict."

I took a deep breath and tried not to incite a different kind of conflict. "So will you have to leave right after the play to write the review?" I asked trying to keep the hope out of my voice.

"No," Dan replied. "I already turned it in. It'll go live online first thing tomorrow."

"How does that work?" Nigel asked taking a sip of his drink. "Isn't tonight the opening night?"

Dan glanced around as if distracted before answering. "Yes, but the days of critics frantically running home to bang out their reviews minutes after the curtain drops have gone the way of the Dodo bird. These days, plays begin well before their so-called opening night. It allows the cast and crew to work out any kinks before it officially opens. Critics are invited late in this preview period when the director thinks the play is ready."

"I never knew that," I admitted as Dan continued to idly scan the room.

At my answer a distinctly patronizing expression crossed his face. "Yes, well, that's not *too* surprising given —" he began, but a sudden movement next to me stopped him. I glanced up at Nigel. Generally, Nigel exudes an air of genial affability wrapped up in a package of absurd good looks. The absurd good looks were still there, but the affability was not. It had been replaced with an almost tangible animosity as he regarded Dan with a challenging stare. Dan blinked at Nigel and quickly looked away. With a faintly apologetic smile, he continued, "Uh . . . given that it's not widely known outside of the theater circle."

"I see. So what was your opinion then?" I asked as I mentally considered options for Dan's recompense. A subscription to several tawdry magazines seemed appropriate. Nigel's reward also contained an element of the tawdry, but in his case it would be appreciated.

Dan stared at me dumbly.

"About Peggy's play?" I prompted. "Did you like it?"

"Oh," he said shifting his feet and averting his eyes. "Yes. Her play. Right. Unfortunately, I'm not allowed to make my opinion known until the review runs. Company policy, I'm afraid." He quickly glanced at us and produced a swift, tight smile. A faint throbbing started behind my right eye. If Dan had disliked Peggy's play and went on to skewer it with his usual venomous style, there'd be no reason for Harper to divorce Dan. She'd just kill him outright.

Six

Harper returned a few minutes later. "Our table is ready," she told us with a bright smile.

Dan turned and stared pointedly at Harper's empty hands. "I thought you went to get me a drink," he said.

The smile faltered. "I did," she said quickly, "but then the hostess said our table was ready. You can order when we are seated."

"Then what took you so long?" he demanded.

Harper flushed and produced an apologetic smile. "I had to use the restroom."

Dan grumbled something, but Harper ignored him. Turning to Nigel and me, she merely said, "Follow me."

With Dan still muttering under his breath, we did. After we were seated and Dan's drink had been ordered, I asked Harper, "Have you talked to Peggy today?"

Harper nodded. "Briefly. She was a mass of nerves. But I told her that we'd see her later tonight after the show."

The producer of Peggy's play, Fletcher Levin, was throwing an after-party at his house for the cast, crew, and their families. As Peggy had insisted that Harper and I were "practically her sisters," we were invited too.

"Speaking of which," Harper continued with a pointed look at Dan, "do not use this party as an excuse to corner Fletcher. This is Peggy's night."

Dan's shoulders stiffened. "Are you serious? Why else do you think I said I'd go to this thing in the first place?"

Harper tried to keep her emotions in check, but I could tell it wasn't easy for her. Hell, even *I* wanted to smack him. "I *thought* you were going to help celebrate the opening night of one of my oldest friend's debut play," she said stiffly.

Dan rolled his eyes. "Look at it as killing two birds with one stone, if it makes you feel any better," he said.

"It doesn't," she bit out.

Dan put his hand palm down on the table. "Come on, Harper, don't be so naive. I've finally found the perfect play to produce. I need investors with deep pockets; investors like Levin. It's not that complicated."

Harper's eyes narrowed. "I never said it was complicated," she bit out. "I said it was *tacky.*"

Dan let out a snort. "Trust me, Levin won't see it that way. He's a businessman. He'll see it for what it is: an amazing investment opportunity."

Harper tried once more. "Dan, please. This is Peggy's night."

Dan threw his hands up in frustration. "So no one can talk about anything else? For Christ's sake, Harper, don't be ridiculous."

"I'm *not.*"

Dan's eyes narrowed. Neither spoke. Finally, Dan blinked and looked at his menu. "Fine. Have it your way. I can't stay long, anyway."

Harper regarded him with a neutral expression. "Oh, and why is that?" she asked.

Dan kept his eyes on the menu. "I have some work I need to do. In fact, I'm going to stay at the apartment tonight."

Harper's mouth pulled down into a slight frown. "I thought you already finished your reviews for tonight," she said.

Dan glanced up from the menu and fixed her with a level look. "I have. But if it hasn't escaped your notice, there are *several* Broadway shows opening this month. Not just Peggy's. Those reviews aren't going to write themselves."

Harper took a deep breath before continuing. "I realize that, but you aren't the only theater reviewer on staff. There's also Zack."

Dan scoffed. "Zack is an Assistant Editor," he said as he resumed his appraisal of the menu. "*I* am the Editor-in-Chief. There's a *big* difference between us."

"Is it ego?" asked Nigel with an innocent expression. When Dan stared at him blankly, Nigel nodded encouragingly. "It is, isn't?" he said.

Harper smothered a smile. "Speaking of Zack," she said. "I told Peggy to invite him to the party as well."

Dan's mouth fell open a little at this. "You told her to invite *Zack*? Why on earth would you do that?" he sputtered.

"I thought it might be a good idea for him to get to know some of that crowd," Harper said. "You've been having him work all hours with you on your book. I thought he deserved a treat."

Dan stared at Harper, his face incredulous. "A treat? What is he, a dog?"

"Of course not," she said, "although you've certainly been working him like one."

Dan gave a grim smile. "Funny, and here I thought I was the one who had been working so hard. Well, since you invited him, you can entertain him. I am not going to change my plans just so I can show Zack a good time."

Harper's nose flared in anger. "Fine," she bit out, "do whatever you want. Just remember you need to be home by ten tomorrow morning."

Dan's brows pulled together. "And why do I need to be home by ten?" he asked.

Harper looked down at her menu. "Because Nic and I are going to brunch."

Dan's brows pulled in even farther. "And?"

Harper's head jerked back as she regarded him with undisguised ire. "*And,* you need to watch Gracie."

Dan made a noise. "Isn't that what we're paying your precious Devin for?"

Harper's lips pressed into a thin line. "Not when she has a perfectly capable *father* who can do it," she said in a low voice.

Dan ignored the barb and stared at his menu. "Who's Devin?" I asked hoping to steer the conversation into more neutral territory.

Harper continued to stare at Dan while she answered me. "Devin is our Nanny. Gracie adores him."

"She's not the only one," Dan muttered.

39

A faint stain crept up Harper's neck. The table fell into an awkward silence.

"Have you always wanted to produce plays, Dan?" I asked after a few moments.

Dan took a sip of his drink before answering. "No, but after covering Broadway for a few years, I realized that if you know what you're doing, you can make a killing by investing in the right play. Granted, it's a risky business and more people fail than not. But if you have the right eye, you can spot a winner."

"And you think you've found a winning play?" I asked.

"I *know* I've found a winning play," Dan corrected. "I didn't get to where I am today at *Vanity Fair* by not knowing what works and what doesn't work. I know what theatergoers will like. In short, I know what plays are destined to be hits."

"What's the play?" I asked.

"*Year with the Yeti*," said Dan. "It's theater gold."

"Interesting title. What's it about?" Nigel asked.

"It's the story of a young man who is orphaned as a small child," Dan said. "Relatives take him in, but he's never really accepted by them. They are narrow-minded, resentful, and content to stay in their little

40

town. The boy, however, wants to see the world and seeks adventure. When the circus comes to the boy's town, he sneaks out to see it. There he meets a magician who offers to show him a different world from the one he is living in. The boy ends up joining the circus and in doing so, finds out who he really is."

"It sounds a bit like *Harry Potter*," I said.

Dan looked at me as if I'd suddenly belched. "I'm sorry," he said. "What?"

"*Harry Potter*," I repeated. "The plot sounds a bit like the basis for Harry Potter. You know, the orphaned boy, the horrible relatives, a magician who shows him another world."

Dan still stared at me in confusion. "The . . . children's books?"

"Well, I don't think they're considered children's books," I began, but Dan cut me off.

"Oh, really?" he sneered. "Then tell me. Were I to go into a bookstore and ask the clerk what section the *Harry Potter* books were housed, where do you think they would direct me? To Classics? To Literature? No, I believe I would be shown to the Young Adult section. Otherwise known as books for *children.*"

I forced myself to smile serenely. It was

either that or stab Dan with my fork. "I take it you're not a fan of the series?" I asked.

"As I am not a child, no," Dan replied curtly before taking a large sip of his drink.

"Oh, you don't know what you're missing," I said, driven by a sophomoric need to needle him. "You really should read them. I've read them all at least three times. I adored them."

Harper now let out a laugh. "That's putting it mildly," she teased. "You were obsessed. I remember for your birthday one year, Peggy and I sent you an acceptance letter from Hogwarts."

I laughed. "I still have it," I said. "But speaking of Harry Potter, did you see *The Cursed Child*? I can't decide if I want to see it. I hate the idea of Harry growing up and becoming a grouchy old man."

Harper shook her head. "I haven't seen it." Turning to Dan, she asked, "Dan, what did you think of it?"

Dan shrugged. "I let Zack review that one," he said with a dismissive sniff. "Like Nic here, he's a fan. Personally, I abhor the current trend of diminishing the line between Hollywood and the theater. It goes against the true spirit of thespianism. I know you work with restoring old films, Nigel, but I think I must say that the cinema is several rungs below theater."

"Well, I can't think of anyone else who would say it," replied Nigel affably.

"It is just that the cinema is crass commercialism intent only on making a profit," Dan continued.

I nodded. "Unlike, say, *Cats,*" I offered.

Nigel affected a look of rapture. "Ah, *Cats.* Now, *that* was a play! Do they still sell the t-shirts? Mine's just about worn out."

Dan stared at Nigel at a loss for words.

SEVEN

"So anyway, there I was in the Algonquin, when who else but Neil Patrick Harris comes in and sees me," said Dan with an affected laugh. "Of course, he insisted on buying me a drink at the bar. He always does."

I stared down at my *steak pomme frites* and willed myself to eat. My appetite had all but disappeared over the last hour as Dan monopolized the conversation with a seemingly endless supply of stories about Broadway. They all shared one purpose; namely, that Dan knew a lot of famous people, and, more importantly, they all thought he was wonderful. Dinner with Dan was nothing more than a sobering interlude of minimum-security imprisonment.

"But then just as Patrick is demanding a bottle of the best champagne they have," Dan went on, "I hear someone calling my name. I turn around and who do you think I see?"

No one answered.

"It's Nathan Lane, of course," said Dan. "And he starts insisting that *he's* buying my drink!"

I set down my fork in defeat. Nigel suddenly reached into the middle of the table and pantomimed picking something up by his fingers. "I believe you dropped another name, Dan," he said, as he pretended to give it back to him.

Dan looked at Nigel in confusion. "What?" he finally said.

"You dropped another name," Nigel repeated. "You might want to be more careful in the future," he added as he eyed the table with pity. "They're scattered all over the tablecloth."

I hid a smile and picked up my fork. My appetite had suddenly returned.

An hour later, we were on our way to the Eugene O'Neill Theater where Peggy's play was opening. Set in the South during the Great Depression, *Dealer's Choice* was the tale of a down-on-his-luck con man, Frankie Davis, whose schemes have ruined his already suffering family. Seasoned actor Jeremy Hamlin had been cast as Frankie, the inept grifter who is convinced his big score is only one "dumb mark" away. Broadway legend Nina Durand played his long-suffering wife, Patsy, who works three jobs to finance her husband's schemes. Up-and-comer Brooke Casey played the wise-beyond-her-years daughter, Lilly, who ultimately proves to have the winning hand. All were excellent in their portrayals, but it was Brooke's steely portrayal of Lilly, a young girl determined to save her family as she outwits the local loan sharks, that stole the show.

Based on the enthusiastic applause from the audience as Brooke took her final bow, I was not alone in my assessment. Harper turned to me, equally excited. "Wasn't she amazing?" she asked me as we both stood for the ovation. "I can't wait to read the reviews — I just know that it's going to be a hit."

I glanced over at Dan as she said this. Like the rest of us, he was on his feet, but his reaction was tepid at best. I didn't think it was because he'd already seen the play, either. My headache, which had vanished during the play, returned.

EIGHT

There are luxury apartments in New York City, and then there are *luxury* apartments. Those found on the Upper West Side are the latter. Many of these block-long condominiums offer not just a place for the super rich to hang their top hat but include such amenities as twelve-screen movie theater complexes, full-service health clubs, and their own post offices. It was in one of these humble abodes that Peggy's producer, Fletcher Levin, resided.

Fletcher Levin was a well-known figure on Broadway, although some might prefer the term "notorious." He had produced and financed numerous plays, and in the process had made an obscene amount of money. There were some who whispered that some of his dealings were underhanded, while others said that they were outright fraudulent. The rumors ranged from defrauding investors to blackmailing actors to rigging

47

award ceremonies.

The building's foyer was an ornate blend of white marble, gold leaf, and mirrored glass. Inside, an unsmiling receptionist checked our names off of a list with the seriousness of a guard at a NATO summit. From there we stepped into a private elevator. The floor was made from reclaimed wood and the walls were padded in tanned leather. A small metal sign next to the control panel read No NOTICES OR FLYERS ALLOWED. Nigel made me take a picture of him standing next to it.

We were whisked with quiet efficiency to the fifty-third floor, where the mirrored doors slid open to reveal a stern-faced butler in a white tuxedo. Our names were once again checked off a list before we were allowed passage through the apartment's oversized mahogany doors. We stepped inside a room with nine-foot ceilings, Brazilian cherry floors, and floor-to-ceiling windows that looked out on Central Park.

I had just been relieved of my coat by a man I hoped was a hired domestic and not a fellow guest when I heard my name being called loudly. I glanced up to see Peggy hurriedly making her way across the crowded room to me, the skirt of her plum-colored gown fluttering behind her. A petite brunette with an hourglass figure and a ready smile, Peggy was a perpetual bundle of motion. Her husband, Evan, the more laidback of the two, trailed in her wake.

"Peggy!" I said with a grin as she pulled me into a hug, "The play was amazing. We loved it."

"Nic! It's so good to see you! Did you really like it? Do you promise?" she asked in a rush, her green eyes shinning with excitement.

Beside her, Evan good-naturedly rolled his eyes. "Peggy, don't be such a goof," he said affectionately. "*Of course* they loved it. How could anyone not?" Tall and lanky with sandy blond hair that flopped over his forehead, Evan was incessantly calm and unflappable. As such he was the perfect foil for Peggy.

"Evan's right," I said. "We loved every second of it." Peggy gave a happy laugh as Nigel and Harper added their compliments. Dan stood impassively to one side, saying nothing.

After hugging both Nigel and Harper, Peggy turned to Dan. Neither pretended a hug was an option for their greeting. "Hello, Dan," Peggy said, her tone now more polite than enthusiastic, "I certainly hoped *you* enjoyed the play."

Dan angled his head in acknowledgment of her statement but said nothing.

Peggy pressed on. "Seriously? All I get is a head tilt? Come on Dan, what did you think of it? It's not like I'm not going to find out," she said with a hopeful smile. "Tell me what you thought."

Dan paused a moment before answering, "It was exactly what I expected."

Evan stiffened. Peggy's smile dimmed. Then with a dismissive shrug, she turned her attention back to Harper and me. "Well, come on everyone," she said. "I want to introduce you to Fletch."

Dan and Harper paused to say hello to a former co-worker, while Nigel and I followed Peggy to the far wall, where our host stood lounging against a piano. Fletcher Levin was a short, bespectacled man of about sixty-five. He had dark brown eyes, the build of a melting snowman, and — based on the few remaining wisps on his head — red hair. In one hand, he held a glass of scotch; in the other, a voluptuous brunette sheathed in red satin. If I had to guess, I'd say the scotch was the older of the two.

"Fletch!" Peggy called out as we approached. "I want you to meet my friends.

This is Nicole Martini and her husband, Nigel."

Fletcher smiled amiably and released his hold on the brunette. "It's always a pleasure to meet a fellow ginger," he said to me. Tapping his bald head, he winked and added, "It's a nice reminder of what used to be here." After greeting Nigel, he turned to the woman at his side, saying, "And this is my friend, Rosie."

"Ruby," the woman corrected, her full lips pulling down into a pout.

"Of course. Forgive me, *Ruby*," Fletcher said smoothly. "It's just that you're as pretty as a rose, and so my tired old brain wants to call you that."

Ruby accepted his apology with a giggle and a simpering smile. Turning to me, she asked, "Are you an actress, too?"

"Oh, no," I answered. "I'm an old friend of Peggy's. We went to school together."

"Oh, that's nice," Ruby replied somewhat absently. Her gaze slid to Nigel. "Are *you* an actor?" she asked hopefully.

Nigel smiled and shook his head. "No, I'm afraid not. But I take it that you are?"

Ruby beamed at him. "I am. And Fletch here says that he might have the perfect role for me in one of his upcoming plays. I'll have lines and everything!" She snuggled closer into Fletch. "Isn't that right, Fletch?"

"Sure is, Rosie," Fletch replied as he took a large sip of his scotch.

"Ruby," she corrected.

"Huh?" he asked.

"It's Ruby."

Fletch gave a self-deprecating roll of his eyes. "Of course it is! *Ruby,*" he repeated, as if trying to commit the name to memory. "I'm sorry, darling, but I'm just terrible with names. But I never forget a face. And yours is too pretty to forget, I can promise you that."

Ruby smiled, somewhat mollified and took a sip of her drink. Fletcher turned his attention back to me. "So you're Peg's college friend. She's been yapping about you nonstop."

"I could say the same about you," I replied.

"Is that so?" he asked, smiling at Peggy. Leaning close to me, he said in a stage whisper, "It's all lies, of course. Don't believe a word of it."

Peggy let out a little laugh. "You don't even know what I told her," she protested.

Fletcher shook his head. "Don't need to. No doubt you said I was a generous, talented, and kind man." He looked to me for corroboration.

I nodded. "That's pretty much what she said." It was a bald-faced lie, of course. Peggy had complained to me numerous times that Fletcher was a micromanaging egomaniac who enjoyed the company of women. "*Young* women," Peggy had added pointedly. "The younger the better, and the *dumber* the better, if you know what I mean." I told her I did.

Peggy now shot me a grateful smile just as Harper joined us. "Oh Harper. There you are," Peggy said. "Harper, I'd like you to meet my producer, Fletcher Levin."

Seeing Harper, Fletcher's expression of polite interest fell away. He stared at her bug-eyed. Tentatively, he reached his hand out to touch her arm and then pulled it back. "Diana?" he whispered.

Harper blinked in surprise. "No, but that was my mother's name," she said.

Fletcher slowly scanned Harper's face. "Your mother was Diana Harrington?"

Harper nodded. "Yes. Well, that was her maiden name. Did you know her?" she asked.

Nodding slowly, he said, "I did. It was many years ago, but I knew your mother very well." He produced an apologetic smile. "Forgive my staring, my dear. It's just uncanny how much you resemble her."

Harper smiled. "That's what everyone tells me. So how did you know my mom?"

Fletcher took a sip of his scotch before answering. "I met your mother the summer before her senior year in college. It was at some country club dance. I was actually there with another girl, but then I saw your mother, and I was a goner. It was love at first sight — well, for me at least." He gave a rueful smile. "I pursued her all summer, rather relentlessly, I'm afraid."

Harper's eyes widened at this. "Really?" She gave a light laugh. "I had no idea. It's funny, you never think of your parents as being with anyone else."

Fletcher shook his head at this. "I didn't say I was successful," he clarified with a regretful sigh. "But I certainly tried my damnedest. Then your father came into the picture, and as they say, that was that."

Harper smiled. "They were very happy," she said.

Fletcher noticed the past verb tense. "Were?" he repeated.

Harper nodded. "Mom died last year," she said, her voice low. "Just after their fortieth wedding anniversary. It was breast cancer."

Fletcher's face fell. "I'm so sorry to hear that," he said. "I had no idea." Pulling his emotions together, he then said, "Well, tell me about yourself, Harper. Are you married?"

Dan joined us just in time to hear this. "She is indeed, sir," he said with an air that suggested Harper had won the marital lottery. "To me. Dan Trados. Perhaps you've heard of me. I'm the theater critic at *Vanity Fair.*" He stuck out his hand. "I've been hoping to meet you for sometime now."

Fletcher stared blankly at Dan and then at Dan's hand and then once again at Dan. His glance finally slid back to Harper, his expression one of hopeful doubt. When Harper nodded her head to indicate the truth of Dan's statement, a faintly horrified expression crept over Fletcher's face. He turned back to Dan and reluctantly shook his hand.

"I've actually been hoping to meet you, Mr. Levin," Dan continued, ignoring the quelling look Harper shot him. "I've come across a play that I think you might be interested in investing in. It's called *Year of the Yeti.*"

Fletcher said nothing.

"The author, Robert Taylor, is an unknown, but he's written a hell of a play," Dan continued. "In fact, I think it's destined to be a hit. It just needs the proper cast and backing."

Again, Fletcher said nothing.

"So anyway, I was hoping that —" Dan's phone suddenly began to chirp. Pulling the device out of his pocket, he glanced down at the readout and frowned. Swiping his thumb across the screen, he angled his body away from us and answered the call. "Hello?" Dan paused to listen. "Oh, right," he said. "Hang on a sec." Turning back to Fletcher, Dan said, "If you will excuse me, Mr. Levin, I need to take this call. I'll be right back." Dan pressed the phone to his ear and quickly walked away.

Fletcher said nothing. He watched him go, his expression that of a man observing a bug crawling across his morning toast.

Turning to Harper, he then offered her his arm. "My dear, perhaps you would be so kind as to walk with me for a moment," he said. "I want to ask you more about your mother."

Harper blinked in surprise but nodded. Fletcher smiled at her and then at us. "If you'll excuse us for a moment," he said. Turning to the all-but-forgotten brunette at his side, he added, "I won't be long, Rosie."

"Ruby," several voices said at once.

NINE

Ruby turned to us with a polite smile. "Well, if you'll excuse me for a moment," she said conversationally, "I've got to pee like a racehorse." No one objected.

As Ruby slowly sashayed away, Peggy watched her, her expression somewhere between bemused and disgusted. "See what I mean about Fletch and the young girls?" she asked. "It's ridiculous. Whatever can she be thinking?"

"I'm going to go with 'vague blurry thoughts,' " I said.

"Don't forget, she's getting a 'real role with lines and everything,' " Nigel added.

Peggy laughed. "Still. She's a pretty girl, and he's old enough to be her grandfather."

I shrugged and sipped my drink. "For some women power is an aphrodisiac."

Nigel nodded in agreement. "Usually for the ones who can't spell *aphrodisiac.*"

Evan clinked his glass against Nigel's in

salute. "God, I've missed you guys," Peggy said. "I know I've been a horrible friend this past year, but I've been just so busy with the play."

"Peggy, don't be silly," I said. "You haven't been a horrible friend. We all understand how time-consuming this was for you. But it was worth it. It's a great play, and it went off without a hitch."

Peggy smiled. "Well, I wouldn't say *that,*" she said. "There were a few bumbles, but nothing major, thank God. Of course, my heart was in my mouth whenever Jeremy was on stage, but I thought he did well tonight."

"Why wouldn't he?" I asked as I glanced over to the man in question. Tall and lanky with dark hair and a long face, Jeremy Hamlin wasn't so much handsome as he was expressive. He had a chameleon-like skill that allowed him to twist and shift his expressions with ease.

Peggy looked at me in surprise. "You mean you don't know?" she asked.

"Apparently not," I admitted.

Peggy leaned close. "About four years ago, Jeremy's work started to get really unpredictable," she said. "He was forgetting his lines, arguing with directors, and generally being a pain in the ass. At the time, everyone thought it was because of his drinking, and less and less people were willing to work with him." She lowered her voice to a whisper, "There was even a rumor going around that he might actually have to quit the theater all together and take a role on" — she glanced furtively around before dramatically hissing — "*General Hospital.*"

I laughed. "Peggy! It's a soap opera, not *cancer.*"

"Well, for *some* people in this crowd, it's a fate worse than cancer . . . or *dinner theatre,*" Peggy averred. "In any case, Jeremy did not want to move to LA. He once said that's where the entrance to hell is." Peggy belatedly realized that Nigel and I lived there and gave an embarrassed laugh. "No offense, of course."

Nigel shook his head. "None taken," he said. "Besides, they moved the entrance a few miles farther south some years back. The property tax out there is sinful, even by Satan's standards."

"Anyway," Peggy continued. "A few months ago, Jeremy came out. He said that he'd been living a lie, and that he had to be true to himself. Of course, everyone was just stunned. We all thought he was such a ladies' man, but it turns out that was all an act."

I looked over to where Jeremy was conducting a rather animated conversation with a small group of people. He flourished his cocktail glass to make a point, sending the amber contents sloshing dangerously close to the edge. A trim blonde in a snug red dress standing next to him warily eyed the glass for a few minutes before deftly removing it from his hand. Jeremy did not appear to notice its absence. "Who's the woman in red?" I asked.

Peggy turned and looked. "Oh, that's Julie Givens, Jeremy's agent. They've been together forever. They're practically joined at the hip. She's the one who finally convinced him to come out. Jeremy was worried that as an openly gay man, he wouldn't be cast in certain roles, but Julie made him see reason. It's a good thing she did, too. The community has been really supportive of him as he works through everything."

Peggy seemed about to say more when something over my right shoulder caught her attention. "Well, this is a surprise! Nina's here," she said. I turned to look where Peggy indicated. Nina Durand stood in the foyer, surveying the mingling guests with an expression that hovered somewhere between bored aristocrat and peevish head-waiter. At five foot four, with ash-blond hair, wide blue eyes, and a milky-white complexion, the comparisons to a Dresden doll were as inevitable as they were laughable, for Nina Durand was nothing if not unabashed in her pursuit of life's earthier pleasures. Child-friendly, she was not.

"Why wouldn't she come?" I asked. "Isn't it customary for the actors to attend their opening night afterparty?"

Peggy tilted her head as she considered my question. "Well, yes. I guess. But Nina is different. She's like Broadway royalty. And she can also be . . . well, Nina can be a bit, um . . . temperamental at times," she finally said.

Beside her Evan bit back a muffled laugh. "More like 'mental,' if you ask me," he said.

Peggy whirled around and glared at him. "Evan! For God's sake, don't! What if she heard you?" she hissed.

Evan's mouth twitched a bit as he glanced down at his irate wife and then to the diminutive woman on the other side of the noisy room. "Then she has bionic ears," he answered. "Besides, I don't think you need to worry. I'd say she's a bit preoccupied at the moment."

We glanced back to where Nina stood. At her side was a young man I guessed to be in his early twenties. He was tall, with blond hair and a trim build. He might have been Nina's son, but I sincerely hoped he was not.

"What the hell is he doing to her?" Evan asked after a minute. "It looks like he's trying to perform CPR on her neck."

"Stop staring," ordered Peggy.

"I can't," Evan complained. "It's like some ghastly car wreck. I can't seem to look away. Oh God. He just licked her ear. Did you see that?"

"I told you not to look," said Peggy.

"Who is he anyway?" Evan asked. "He's got to be at least half her age."

Peggy arched her eyebrow. "And that age discrepancy didn't bother you when it was between Fletch and Ruby, why?"

Evan quickly arranged his face into a contrite expression. "Because I employ a double standard when it comes to judging women, of which I am heartily ashamed, and will work toward improving," he dutifully recited.

"That's what I thought," Peggy replied with a smile. "Anyway, *that's* Nina's flavor of the week," she said as she jerked her chin toward the young man. "There's no point in learning his name. There will be a new one in his place before you know it. If I've learned anything by working with Nina Durand it's that she rather enjoys the company of men."

"Is it true that she and Fletcher were once an item?" Even asked.

"Lower your voice," Peggy admonished. "But to answer your question, yes, they once were an item. They were even briefly engaged."

"When was this?" I asked.

"At least twenty years ago," said Peggy. "Nina was just starting her career. She couldn't have been more than eighteen."

"What happened?" Evan asked.

Peggy shrugged. "I don't know. But whatever it was, it ended badly. Nina took a year-long hiatus somewhere in Europe. When she came back, she wanted nothing to do with Fletcher." Peggy was quiet a moment as she watched Nina and her young friend. "Nina seems to prefer variety rather than a steady relationship, so perhaps that had something to do with it."

Nigel gave a knowing laugh. "That's true. Nina likes her men like Kleenex; strong yet disposable."

"Oh," said Peggy turning to him. "Do you know her?"

"We've met," Nigel said with an evasive shrug. "However, I don't believe Nic has had the pleasure."

I glanced up at Nigel, eyebrow raised. "No, I haven't, but I'm certainly curious to hear about yours."

"My what?" Nigel asked.

"Pleasure," I said.

Nigel winked. "Darling, you know a gentleman doesn't kiss and tell."

"I do indeed, which is why I'm asking *you*," I replied.

Nigel let out a lusty sigh. "You wound me. What can I say? It was spring and a young man's fancy lightly turns to . . ."

I cut him off. "Yes. I'm well acquainted with what your fancy lightly turns to."

Nigel leaned down and kissed my cheek. "I promise you, darling, you're the only girl I've ever truly fancied."

A waiter in a white jacket passed by, and Peggy neatly lifted a glass of champagne from his tray. "Come with me," she said, as we took a glass as well. "I should say hello to Nina."

We crossed the room to where the famed actress stood. Up close, her features seemed somehow exaggerated; her blue eyes were a bit more prominent, her mouth a little wider. She wore a strapless gown of ice blue satin. Glittering crystals adorned the low-cut neckline, highlighting the generous cleavage found there.

Nina smiled fondly at Peggy. "Peggy, darling," she said in her trademark throaty voice. "Tell me, were you pleased? *I* thought it was a smashing success. Toby here thought so, too," she said absentmindedly gesturing at the young man at her side. Toby gave a dutiful nod. "In fact, my only complaint is that I don't have a drink," Nina continued. "Please tell me you brought me one. I'm beyond parched."

Peggy blinked. "I'm sorry, Nina," she sputtered. "I didn't think to get you one."

Nina shrugged and deftly plucked Peggy's champagne flute from her fingers. "Never mind, darling. This will do." In a flash, the glass was raised and drained. "Ugh. It tastes like something you'd buy at a drugstore," she sniffed. "God, Fletch has lousy taste." Nina's gaze suddenly landed on Nigel. A slow smile spread across her face. Thrusting the now empty glass at Toby, she said, "Darling, be a dear and go get me another one, will you?"

"But I thought you didn't like it," Toby protested.

"*Now,* darling."

"Of course, Nina," Toby said as he scampered off in search of a waiter.

"Nina," said Peggy. "I'd like to introduce you to some friends of mine. This is . . ."

65

"Nigel Martini," Nina said with a throaty purr. Stretching her hand out, she slowly trailed one red fingernail down his lapel. "You sly bastard, I haven't seen your handsome face in ages."

Nigel laughed as he deftly removed her hand and briefly kissed it before releasing it. "Hello, Nina," he said. "It's good to see you. How have you been?"

Nina moistened her lips. "Oh, you know," she said with a slight flick of her wrist. "Working keeps me pretty busy, but I manage to make time for some fun. How about you? Are you still breaking hearts out in LA?"

Nigel shook his head. "No. Those days are over. I married a lovely girl, adopted a dog, and settled down."

Nina tilted her head back, exposing her long white neck, and let out a throaty laugh. The gesture reminded me of something you'd see in one of those nature programs Nigel and I watch when we can't find the remote; the ones that depict the savage beauty of an animal before it attacks.

"Oh Nigel, I'd forgotten how funny you are," she said her voice almost a purr. She lifted her hand and trailed her long fingers slowly down her throat before extending them towards Nigel's chest. "It seems like just yesterday that you and I were . . ."

I intercepted the hand. Giving it a firm shake, I said in a cheerful voice, "Hello, Ms. Durand. I'm Nic Martini, Nigel's wife. It's a pleasure to meet you."

Nina stared at my hand, then at me, and then at Nigel. I felt her grip go slack and she released my hand. "Wait, you were serious?" she asked Nigel. "You really got married?"

"I really got married," Nigel confirmed, wrapping his arm around my shoulders. With a grin he added, "I'm respectable now."

"Well, I wouldn't go that far," I said.

Nina's surprised glance shifted back to me; her gaze quickly flicked up and down my body. "Well, well. Nigel Martini married," she said, producing a wide smile. "I never thought I'd live to see the day. You must be an extraordinary woman."

"She most certainly is," Nigel agreed affably as he lightly kissed my temple.

Nina arched an eyebrow. "Does that mean you really own a dog?" she asked. "Whatever for?"

I shrugged. "Well, sometimes Nigel gets lonesome."

Nigel laughed and kissed me again.

"Nic and I went to college together,"

Peggy added. "I think I told you about her."

Nina's eyes widened slightly at this. "Wait. You're not the one who used to be a cop, are you?" she asked.

"Detective," I corrected. "But yes. That's me."

Nina glanced briefly at Peggy, before saying to me, "I must confess, you're not at all what I expected. When Peggy told me her old college friend was coming and that she used to be a cop —" She paused and corrected herself. "I'm sorry, *a detective,* but that she'd been shot a few years back and had to retire, I pictured some disabled sourpuss with a bad haircut. Or at the very least, like one of the horrible nuns I had in Catholic school. But you're nothing like that!"

"Thank you," I said. "I think."

Nina laughed. "You're right. That did sound terrible, didn't it? Not setting the bar for improvement terribly high, was I? But you're lovely." She patted my hand and added, "And I'm not just saying that because it's what I say to everyone I meet. I actually mean it."

I smiled. "And, may I say, that I think *you're* lovely, too."

Nina paused and stared at me for a beat before letting out a peal of laughter. "Oh, I like her, Nigel. I really do. I can see why you married her."

Toby returned now with Nina's glass of champagne. "Thank you, darling," she said to him as she took the glass. Raising her arm, she added, "Well, I think a toast is in order. To Peggy and her *lovely* play, and to Nigel and his *lovely* bride. To new beginnings! Cheers!"

"Well, if it isn't the *lovely* Nina!" Fletcher's voice suddenly boomed out from behind me. "I thought I heard you. But of course, you do tend to project even when off-stage. Remember, dear, as I always say, *less* is *more*."

Nina slowly angled her head to look at Fletcher as she took a leisurely sip of her champagne. "Would that were only true for *all* aspects of life," she said with a sigh, as she lifted up her glass and stared directly at his crotch. "How happier we'd all be."

TEN

We were spared of any more poisonous offerings of advice or trips down a memory lane ridden with landmines by the appearance of Harper. With her was a young man of about thirty-five, who I assumed was Dan's assistant, Zack. He had a plump, owlish face, round tortoiseshell glasses, and a shock of coal black hair. If Harper noticed the tension within our little group, she didn't let on. But then Harper had years of practice of defusing awkward social situations from her marriage to Dan. Adroitly stepping between Nina and Fletch, she smiled brightly at the latter and said, "Mr. Levin, I wanted to introduce you to Zack Weems, Dan's assistant."

Fletcher nodded politely. Zack put out his hand, saying, "It's an honor to meet you, sir. Your generosity has made the theater what it is today."

"Well, that's very kind of you to say, son,"

Fletcher said. "Of course, I don't expect my lifelong support of the arts to be singled out for special praise, but it is nice to be recognized." Here Fletcher paused and smiled as if to give the rest of us a chance to add our own praise. No one did. After a second, he blinked and returned his attention to Zack. "So your name is Zack Weems? And you're with *Vanity Fair*?" Zack nodded. "And have you always wanted to be a theater critic?" Fletcher asked.

"Yes," said Zack. "Although one day I'd love to write plays rather than review them."

"A fine goal," said Fletcher. "Have you written anything yet?"

Zack shrugged. "I've been working on something for a few years now, but I'm not sure if it's ready for prime time yet."

"Well," said Fletcher, "I'll be sure to keep an eye out for you. You seem like a capable young man."

Gesturing to a hovering waiter, Fletcher held up two fingers. The waiter nodded and left only to return moments later with two tumblers. Fletcher took both and handed one to Zack. "Welcome to my house, Zack."

"Thank you, sir," Zack said as he took the glass.

Fletcher clinked his glass to Zack's. "Cheers."

Zack took a hesitant sip of his drink and pulled a face. "Something wrong?" asked Fletcher.

Zack swallowed and sheepishly shook his head. "No. It's just I'm not a big whiskey drinker," he said.

Fletcher laughed. "Good to hear it. Neither am I. Can't stand the stuff really. That's why *this* is scotch," he said lifting the glass in a salute.

"Oh, right. Sorry," Zack said. "I guess I haven't quite gotten to the point where I like it. My dad always said that if you drink scotch before you're forty, you're an idiot, but if you don't drink it after you're forty, you're an even bigger idiot."

Nigel laughed. "I think that actually might be on my family's coat of arms," he said.

Fletcher gave a good-natured shrug. "Well, if you don't want it, I'll take it," he said. Reaching out, he swiftly took the glass from Zack and dumped the contents into his own.

Nina gave a snort of disgust. "Classy, Fletch. Real classy," she scoffed.

Fletcher's eyes narrowed and his mouth pinched. Nina smirked and raised her eyebrows in an unspoken challenge. Harper interceded before the spat could continue. "Nina," she suddenly said, "I wanted to tell you, I thought you were *amazing* tonight, simply amazing. How have you been?"

Nina appeared caught off guard by Harper's interruption. Glancing away from Fletcher, she produced a thin smile and said, "That's kind of you to say, Harper. I've been well. How have you been?"

"I've been good," Harper said. "For the most part. Gracie is wonderful, but it's definitely been an adjustment. Half the time I walk around with baby mush brain. I think that's the worst part, don't you?"

A faint line appeared between Nina's eyes. "Don't I what?" she repeated slowly.

"Think that baby mush brain is the worst part," Harper said.

Nina stared at Harper. "I really wouldn't know," she said stiffly.

Harper's eyes grew wide and her face flushed with embarrassment. "Oh God, of course you don't. Just ignore me," she said with an awkward laugh. "But in case anyone needed an example of what I'm talking about, this is it. Baby mush brain at its finest. I don't know what I'm saying half the time."

Nina stared at her for a beat. "So you and Dan had a baby?" she finally said slowly.

Harper nodded. "Yes. Well, technically, I did. Her name is Gracie. She's six months old, and I love her to bits, but what I wouldn't give to sleep though the night again and not be covered in spit-up."

Nina blinked. Her expression was one of faint confusion and disgust. Not unlike the reaction Nigel has when we run out of scotch. "How lovely," Nina said, her voice faint. "Congratulations." Her gaze slid from Harper to Zack.

"Oh, excuse me," said Harper. "Nina, this is Zack Weems. He works with Dan at *Vanity Fair.*"

Nina smiled politely and extended her hand to Zack. "Very nice to meet you, Zack," she said. Then with a thoughtful tilt of her head, she added, "So what's it like to work with Dan?"

"It's been very educational," Zack said with a diplomatic smile.

"I can only imagine," Nina murmured.

"Speaking of which, where is Dan?" asked Harper.

"On a phone call, I believe," said Peggy as she extended her hand to Zack. "Hi, I'm Peggy McGrath."

Zack smiled and shook her hand. "Congratulations on your play," he said. "I've been hearing great things about it."

Peggy smiled. "From Dan, I hope?"

Zack's smile slipped slightly. "Oh, well, I

haven't seen Mr. Trados's final review yet, but a few other people I've spoken with had nothing but praise. I haven't had a chance to see it myself yet, unfortunately, but I'm hoping to next week."

Peggy was saying something about sending over a ticket to his office, when a faint commotion in the foyer caught Zack's attention. His eyes grew wide, his expression reverent. "Oh my God," he said. "I think I just died and went to heaven."

ELEVEN

Heaven, apparently, was Brooke Casey. The up-and-coming actress was only twenty-three, but she was already making quite a name for herself. She'd won a Tony last year and thanks to her quick wit she was something of a darling of the late-night talk shows. She was also undeniably gorgeous with long blond hair, bright blue eyes, and the body of a lingerie model. The latter was artfully displayed in a buttery yellow gown that clung to her every curve.

"She does seem to have that effect on men," said Peggy as she smiled at Zack's reaction. "I think just about every heterosexual male involved in the play had a crush on her by the time we were done with rehearsals."

"Who's that with her?" I asked, indicating the man at her side. He was a good deal older than Brooke, with sharp features, an athletic build, and an easy smile.

"That's Mark Abbot," said Peggy. "The play's director."

I glanced back at the couple, noting the way Mark kept his hand on the small of Brooke's back as they made their way through the crowd. "I take it that Mark has a crush on Brooke as well?" I asked.

Peggy laughed. "No. Mark's flat out in love with her. I think everyone knows it, too, except for Brooke. But in her defense, I guess when everybody falls a little in love with you, it's hard to know when it's something more serious."

Brooke and Mark slowly made their way across the room to where we stood. Seeing Peggy, Brooke's face broke out into a bright smile. "Peggy!" Brooke said, as she pulled her into a tight hug, "I think you have a hit on your hands! I can't thank you enough for casting me. It's a dream role."

Peggy waved away the compliment. "Don't be silly," she said. "I'm the one who should be thanking you. There's no one else who could play Lilly. If the play's a hit then a great deal of the credit must go to you." Turning, Peggy quickly added, "And to you as well, Mark. Tonight's production was flawless."

Mark let out a good-natured laugh as he leaned in to kiss Peggy's cheek. "That's a load of crap, Peg, and you know it. No production is ever flawless. But I will agree with you that Brooke's performance tonight *was*." Mark looked down at Brooke with obvious affection. "I predict she's on her way to winning another Tony."

Brooke blushed prettily. "Mark and I had a celebratory glass of champagne in the limo on the way here," she said, as if embarrassed by his flattery. "I think it's gone to his head."

Mark shook the appendage in question. "I'm not that big of a lightweight," he said. "You were amazing tonight. You'll see, the reviews will prove me right."

Brooke blushed again before glancing curiously at Harper and me. Turning her attention back to Peggy, she said, "So are these your friends from college you were telling me about?"

Peggy nodded and made the introductions. Brooke was happily chatting about the play when Dan returned. "Zack," he said, his voice bored, "I suppose you've met everyone."

Zack nodded. "Yes, we've been chatting about the play," he said.

Dan, however, was no longer paying attention to his colleague. His focus had shifted to Brooke. "You're looking lovely as always, Brooke," he said with a strangely intimate smile. "Wonderful performance tonight, by the way. I have to admit when I first heard that you'd been cast as Nina's daughter, I didn't think it would be believable."

Nina interrupted with a little laugh. "Well, of course not," she said with a wink. "I'm far too young."

Dan shifted his gaze to Nina and raised one eyebrow. Nina flushed angrily. With a faint smirk, Dan turned back to Brooke. "Well, in any case, you gave an excellent performance," he said.

If Brooke noticed the flirtatious tone in Dan's voice, she ignored it. "How kind of you to say," she said politely and then turned to talk with Mark. Dan, however, continued to focus on Brooke. He maneuvered himself so that he was standing next to her and took every opportunity to touch her arm or shoulder or hand. Harper watched his incessant flirting with an expression I couldn't quite pinpoint; it was somewhere between hurt, resigned, and pensive. Mark's reaction to Dan's behavior was much easier to read. He looked like he wanted to punch him in the face. As for Brooke, she seemed unaffected; in fact, she almost seemed oblivious. I was beginning to think that Brooke was simply accustomed to men flirting with her, when Dan rested his hand on the small of her back as he leaned in close to her under the pretense of hearing her better. Brooke's nostrils flared in obvious annoyance. A second later, the contents of her wineglass were dripping down the front of Dan's pants.

"Oh, I am so sorry!" Brooke said, her eyes large with embarrassment.

"I'm such a klutz!"

"It's fine," Dan muttered as he attempted to mop up the mess with his cocktail napkin.

"Oh, that'll never work," protested Brooke. "We need to get you a towel or something."

"A fine idea," Fletcher said, his voice sounding suspiciously like he was trying not to laugh. "I believe there are some hand towels in the bathroom, Dan. Why don't you check there?"

Perhaps hearing the same suppressed laughter that I had, Dan glanced sharply at the older man. With a curt nod, he said, "Thanks, I'll do that."

With a rueful shake of her head, Brooke apologized again. The movement sent her hair tumbling over her shoulders. "I really am sorry, Mr. Trados," she said. "Please make sure to send me the dry cleaning bill."

Dan grunted something at her before

making his way to the bathroom. Brooke turned back to the group, but not before I saw her shoot a quick wink in Nina's direction.

Twelve

"The reviews are in!" Peggy cried sometime later. She thrust her phone at Evan, saying, "You have to read them. I'm too nervous."

Evan took the phone and began to scroll as Harper and I crowded behind him, trying to read over his shoulder. "Check *The Times*, first," Peggy said as she sat down in a nearby chair. She nervously chewed on her thumbnail while Evan pulled up the site. As his dark eyes scanned the readout, a smile tugged at his mouth. "It's good news, Peg. You can leave your thumb alone. They loved it. Listen, '*Dealer's Choice* is a touching story with a superb cast. Jeremy Hamlin shines as Frankie Davis, a down-on-his-luck grifter. Nina Durand and Brooke Casey have a natural chemistry in their respected roles of mother and daughter. Ms. Durand brings real pathos to the role of Frankie's wife, Patsy, and Ms. Casey is marvelous as his daughter Lilly. Ms. McGrath's debut is sure to please theater goers of all ages.' "

Peggy gave a squeal of excitement and jumped out of the chair. Grabbing the phone from Evan's hand, she peered down at the screen to read for herself. "Oh my God!" she said. "It's true! They really did like it!"

Evan rolled his eyes. "Well, of course they did. You think I'd make up a fake review?"

Peggy didn't answer; she kept scrolling through the phone. She let out another happy shriek, saying, "Listen to this! *Variety* called it, 'Eloquent, moving, and exquisitely toned. A sure hit!' " Peggy executed a little happy dance and then scrolled some more. "And here's Dan's review!" she said as she began to read. However, within seconds Peggy's smile faded and her mouth opened in surprise.

A faint line appeared between Evan's eyes. "What does it say, Peg?"

Peggy raised her head, her glance briefly landing on Nina. Just as quickly, she looked away. "Oh. Right. Sorry," she replied to Evan with a quick smile. "Dan said, 'Ms. McGrath's debut play, *Dealer's Choice,* is a charming and wry tale of the boundaries of family obligation. Famed producer, Fletcher Levin, invested a considerable amount of money in the production, and his efforts

83

have paid off. Under Mark Abbot's nuanced direction, the actors' struggles become our own. Jeremy Hamlin delivers a masterful performance as Frankie Davis, a grifter trying to better his family.' " Peggy paused as if she was skipping over something, and then continued. "Brooke Casey steals the show with a natural grace and elegance seldom seen in an actress her age. Ms. Casey delivers an astonishing performance as the young ingénue, Lilly Davis, who is forced to save her father and her family. Broadway certainly has a new star on its horizon.' "

Peggy looked up and clicked off her phone with a bright smile. "Great job everyone," she said. "I'm so proud of all of you and more grateful than you'll ever know."

Nina regarded Peggy, her expression thoughtful. After a moment, she pulled out her own phone and began to scroll through it. Peggy saw her and sought to distract her. "I know! Let's get a photo of everyone," Peggy said. "Can we do that?" Tossing her phone to Evan, she continued in an overly bright voice. "Evan? Will you take the picture? Come on, everyone. Gather round!"

However, before anyone could move, Nina's distinctive voice rang out. " 'Broadway staple Nina Durand once again proves that she can act, but that she's better at overacting,' " Nina read from her phone. " 'Unlike a fine wine that improves with age, Ms. Durand has not, although no one can accuse her of not trying. Ms. Durand's portrayal of Patsy Davis is cartoonish at best.' " Her words effectively silenced those around her. Nina slowly raised her head from her phone and looked around the room for Dan. He was standing in the room's far corner in a conversation with Zack, seemingly unaware of Nina's ire. Her eyes narrowed and she took a step in his direction. Peggy's arm shot out in an attempt to stop her, but Nina shrugged her off.

"Nina, who cares what he thinks?" Peggy said. "He's a jerk. Everyone knows that. It's just one review. Everyone else loved it." Next to me, I heard Harper's sharp intake of breath. I snuck a glance at her. Her face was white with anger but she said nothing.

"No," Nina said in a low voice, her gaze still on Dan. "He went out of his way to be nasty. This isn't a review; it's a personal attack. So now I'm going to do the same. After all, turnabout is fair play."

Some long dormant sense of self-preservation seemed to come alive within Dan.

With a slow turn of his head, he scanned the room, his eyes landing almost immediately on Nina. A flash of some emotion I couldn't quite identify flickered across his face before he erased it with a smug smile. Nina stomped across the room until she was standing right in front of Dan. "Who the hell do you think you are, you lousy son-of-a-bitch?" she hissed as she jabbed her finger into his chest.

Dan said nothing. Next to him, Zack slowly backed away. Neither Nina nor Dan seemed to notice. "Say something, you lousy son-of-a-bitch!" Nina yelled.

Dan smirked. "You already called me that. Perhaps your limited vocabulary is part of your acting problem —"

Dan got no further than that before Nina slapped him across the face. Hard. Dan blinked but did not move. After a painful moment in which it seemed the entire room was frozen in shock, Dan gave a slight nod of his head. "And this would be an example of the overacting I mentioned."

"Go to hell, Dan," Nina said. "You're nothing but a —"

"Yes, I know," said Dan, cutting her off. "A lousy son-of-a-bitch. I believe you've already made that point. However, I do agree that perhaps it's time for me to leave. I seem to have put a damper on your celebration." With a quick move, Dan drained the rest of his drink and set his empty glass on a nearby table. Walking to Harper, he said, "I'll be at the apartment if you need me."

Harper said nothing. She stared at Dan as if she were looking at a stranger. Dan shrugged and leaned in to kiss her cheek, but Harper pulled away before he could do so. "Right. So goodnight then," Dan said, as if she hadn't just snubbed him. "I'll see you tomorrow."

THIRTEEN

"Nigel, I'm already late!" I said as I gently slapped his hand away from my waist.

"That's not my fault," he replied as his hand purposefully snaked back to my hip.

I paused in buckling the ankle strap on my black suede pump and glanced over my shoulder to where he still lay sprawled on the bed. Raising an eyebrow, I shot him a meaningful look. He grinned and said, "Okay, maybe I had *something* to do with it. But really, who schedules brunch for ten o'clock in the morning? What are they, farmers?"

I laughed. "Well, you needn't let it worry you. Go back to sleep and I'll take you to a proper brunch when I return."

Nigel smiled. "I've got a better idea. How about we —" he began just as my cell phone rang.

"Will you answer that, honey?" I said as I finished buckling the strap. "If that's Harper, tell her I'll be there in fifteen minutes."

Nigel rolled over onto his stomach and reached for the phone. Pulling the receiver to his ear, he said, "You've reached the phone of Nicole Martini. This is her house-boy, Juan, how may I help you?"

I threw a pillow at his head and went in search of the other shoe. I vaguely remembered it being flung in the direction of the bathroom. I began to walk/hop over that way when Nigel's next words stopped me. "Whoa, calm down, Harper. I can't understand you. What happened?"

I turned back to where Nigel was now sitting bolt upright in the bed, a line of worry etched between his eyes. I could hear Harper's agitated voice on the other end of the line, but I couldn't make out her words. Nigel's eyes widened as he listened, and he glanced at me. Flipping off the sheets, Nigel stood up and walked toward the room's desk. Yanking open the drawer, he pulled out a pad of hotel stationary and a pen. "Harper, honey, listen to me," he said, his voice calm. "I need you to give me the address."

After writing down the information, Nigel said, "Now Harper, I want you to call the police. Now. Nic and I will be there as soon as possible. In the meantime, don't touch anything. Do you understand? Touch nothing. In fact, why don't you go outside and wait for us there? Okay? Okay, honey. We're on our way." Nigel ended the call and turned to me.

"What's going on?" I asked. "Is Harper okay?" I covered my mouth with my hand as another thought presented itself. "Oh God, it's not the baby is it? Please tell me Gracie is okay."

"Harper is fine and so is Gracie," Nigel said as he grabbed a pair of jeans from the closet and pulled them on. "It's Dan, I'm afraid."

"Dan?" I repeated dumbly.

Nigel nodded as he shrugged into a shirt. "He didn't show up this morning to watch Gracie. When Harper couldn't get ahold of him, she got worried and went to his apartment." Crossing over to me, Nigel pulled me close. "He's dead, Nic."

FOURTEEN

Every New Yorker knows that when you don't need a cab, twenty available ones will pass your way. It's when you desperately need one that they suddenly become scarce. However, when you desperately need one *and* you are traveling with a 120-pound Bullmastiff, you might as well be standing in the middle of the street covered in blood and holding a knife. Fortunately, Nigel managed to flag one down and convince him that Skippy was an excellent tipper before he could take off. Unfortunately, by the time we got to Dan's weekend apartment, the police had already arrived and secured the scene.

I looked for Harper amid the crowd of curious bystanders, police, and paramedics, but didn't see her. However, I did see someone else I knew: my ex-partner Marcy Garcia.

"Marcy!" I called out as I made my way

over to the petite brunette. At the sound of my voice, she spun around. Seeing me, she smiled and made her way over, her smile growing wider when she saw Nigel and Skippy.

"Nic!" she said, giving me a quick hug, "what are you doing here? I didn't even know you were in town."

I waited until Marcy had said hello to Nigel and Skippy before explaining our presence. "A friend of mine's play opened on Broadway last night," I explained. "So Nigel and I . . ."

Marcy's eyes narrowed as soon as she heard me say *Broadway*. "Stop right there," she said holding up her hand. "You being here wouldn't have anything to do with the reason *I'm* here, now would it?"

I gave a small smile. "Well, that all depends. Any chance you're *not* here because of a deceased theater critic?"

Marcy blew out an annoyed breath. "Dammit, Nic. How do you know Dan Trados?"

"I went to school with his wife, Harper," I explained. "She's the one who called me, actually. We were supposed to meet for brunch this morning. Speaking of which, any idea where she is? I'd like to talk to her."

Marcy nodded. "She's talking with my

partner now. And speaking of *him,* he's a good guy, but he's strictly by the book."

"So? I was strictly by the book," I said.

Marcy made a noise that sounded suspiciously like a scoff. "Um, A, you never were by the book," she said. "B, you're no longer on the force, and C, you never were by the book."

"You already said that," I pointed out.

Marcy nodded. "I'm aware of that. Some things bear repeating."

"I just want to talk to her, Marcy. She's an old friend, and she called me."

Marcy closed her eyes and sighed. "Fine. As long as *all* you do is talk to her. I don't want a repeat of what happened with Nigel's family last year."

Last year, Nigel's Aunt Olive had asked for my help with a missing person case. Actually, she didn't ask for my help; she demanded it. Aunt Olive is not a woman who leaves anything to chance. The missing person was her son-in-law, Leo. Unfortunately, Leo was one of those men who are better off left missing. Against my better judgment, I agreed to find him. That little adventure resulted in the discovery of three murders and a firm desire to avoid Martini family gatherings for a while.

"Hey!" Nigel now said with feigned indignation. "They're Nic's family now, too, even if only by marriage."

I stared at him in mock horror and shook my head. "No. No, they're not. You take that back *right* now."

Marcy breathed out her nose. "I don't care *whose* family they are. I just don't want a repeat of last year."

"But we did solve the case," I pointed out.

"Yes, but the Captain still sat me down for a very long chat about professional boundaries. I'd really rather not have to go through that again. I don't think I need to remind *you* about how painful his chats can be."

I nodded grimly. "No, I still remember those chats quite well. I promise that the Captain won't have any reason to be upset."

"Yeah, well, don't take this the wrong way, but I'll believe it when I see it," Marcy said. With a pointed glance at Skippy, she asked, "He won't contaminate my crime scene will he?"

"Who?" I asked.

"Skippy," Marcy clarified.

I shook my head. "Oh, no. Don't worry. He's been trained to keep his paws to himself."

Marcy nodded. "Good."

I lowered my voice. "I was worried for a

minute you were talking about Nigel."

Hearing this, Nigel playfully smacked my rear end. I turned back to Marcy. "See what I mean?" I said.

FIFTEEN

Dan's "grubby weekend office" was located in a gleaming tower smack in the middle of the Theater District. Marcy led us past the concierge and to a row of elevators. From there we rode in silence to the tenth floor. Dan's apartment was at the end of the carpeted hallway. I took a quick look around, noting the hardwood floors, high ceilings, separate kitchen with updated granite countertops and wood cabinets, as well as a private terrace. The décor was high-end and decidedly masculine; the black leather couch, faux fur rugs, and sleek steel tables, while stylish, were far too modern for Harper's taste. This was no dingy hole-in-the-wall where Dan could find some quite time to complete his reviews. This was an expensive second home made for entertaining. Right now, it was being combed over for evidence by Forensics.

Harper was sitting in the kitchen at a glass

table, staring vacantly at her hands; she did not appear to notice our arrival. Her face was pale and splotchy, and her eyes were red and puffy. Across from her, sat a man I guessed to be in his late thirties. He had broad shoulders close-cropped black hair, and the carefully shuttered expression of an experienced detective. Something about the way he tapped on the battered spiral notebook on his lap filled me with unease.

I tugged twice on Marcy's sleeve and tilted my head questioningly when she looked at me. We'd been together long enough that she didn't need to ask what I wanted to know. "He's in the bedroom," she murmured. "The medical examiner is in there with him now."

"Any idea what happened?" I asked.

Marcy shrugged before answering. "From the looks of it, it seems to be either a drug overdose or some kind of poison. Either way, it didn't appear to be a peaceful death."

"So you don't think it was suicide?"

Marcy shook her head. "No. For one thing, there wasn't a note." Glancing around the apartment, she added, "And I have a feeling that he wasn't the kind of guy to let his views go unheard."

"Oh no," I agreed. "No shyness there. Dinner parties might never be the same."

Marcy glanced over at Harper. "So what was their relationship like?"

I paused. "They had their ups and downs like any couple," I hedged. Marcy's slow eyebrow raise indicated what she thought of my answer. "That's your new partner?" I asked, indicating the man sitting with Harper.

Marcy rolled her eyes at my change of subject but nodded. "Yep. That's Brian."

"You like him?"

Marcy shot me a level look. "We have our ups and downs just like any couple," she said.

"Okay," I conceded. "Touché. Dan could be a pompous ass at times and I think he cared more about his career than he did Harper."

Marcy nodded thoughtfully for a moment and then said, "Brian is a good guy. He's very thorough. He can be a stickler for rules though, which is a new experience for me," she added archly.

"Is Harper a suspect?" I asked suddenly.

Marcy blew out a sharp breath through her nose. "It's too early to start talking about that, Nic," she said.

I shot her a meaningful look. "Come on, Marcy," I pressed. "It's me. You and I knew within two minutes if we thought someone was a suspect. What's the story?"

Marcy gave a reluctant shrug. "Well, if it turns out that he was poisoned, then she's . . . well, let's just say she'd be a person of interest."

"Shit, Marcy," I said. "Dan wasn't the most likable man, but I know Harper. She's not a killer."

"Well, then she has nothing to worry about," Marcy replied cryptically.

"Thanks," I said. "That's very reassuring. What about Brian, though?"

"What about him?"

"Does he think Harper is a killer?"

As if he heard me, Brian blinked up at me and frowned. After murmuring something to Harper, he got up from the table and crossed over to where we all stood.

"Who are you and why are you here?" he asked.

"I like a man who gets to the point," Nigel said, sticking out his hand. "I'm Nigel Martini and this is my wife, Nic. We're friends of Harper's."

"Mrs. Trados called them when she discovered her husband," Marcy explained quickly, her voice low. In a slightly louder voice, she then added, "Nic, Nigel, this is my partner, Detective Brian Johnson."

Brian gave Nigel and me a perfunctory

handshake before turning his attention back to Marcy. "I haven't finished talking to Mrs. Trados yet," he said in a low voice. "Perhaps her *friends* can wait outside until we're done. I really don't think —" Brian suddenly stopped and looked down. Skippy had planted himself at Brian's feet and was now repeatedly and enthusiastically smacking his paw on the man's thigh.

"He wants you to shake his paw," Nigel explained. "Whenever he sees us shake hands, he thinks he needs to as well. We may have been a bit overzealous about that part of his training."

Brian stared at Nigel and then at Marcy. She gave him a slight shrug. "Uh, okay," he said, extending his hand down to grip Skippy's paw. Skippy gave a happy bark.

"I am sorry to barge in on your interview, Detective Johnson," I said. "And I promise I won't interfere. But Harper is one of my oldest friends, and I just want to make sure she's okay."

Brian started to shake his head. "I appreciate that ma'am, but . . . wait, did you say your name is Nic Martini? As in Marcy's old partner?" he asked.

"That's me, although I prefer 'ex-partner,'" I said with a smile.

Brian did not return my smile. Instead, he

opened his mouth and then abruptly shut it. Turning to Marcy, he jerked his head toward the front hallway and said, "Can I talk to you for a second, Marcy?"

Marcy sighed. "Sure, Brian."

While the two of them engaged in a rather tense, hushed conversation, I took the opportunity to go over to Harper. She was still sitting at the kitchen table with a blank expression on her face. "Hey, Harper," I said as I drew near. I pulled up a chair and sat down next to her. Taking one of her hands in mine, I asked, "How're you doing, honey?"

Harper shook her head and her eyes filled with fresh tears. "He's gone, Nic. I don't understand. This doesn't make sense."

"I'm so sorry, Harper," I said, gently squeezing her hand. "Is there anything we can do?"

Harper stared at me blankly. "He's dead. Dan is dead."

I nodded slowly and glanced at Nigel. "Any chance one of the paramedics can come inside for a minute?" I asked. "I think she might be in shock."

Nigel nodded and quickly walked outside. I turned back to Harper. "It's going to be okay, Harper," I said. "Why don't I make you a cup of tea or something?" I stood up and began to rummage through the cabinets until I found what I was looking for. "Do you want Earl Grey, Darjeeling, Black, or Green?" I asked reading from the various boxes.

Harper stared at me in confusion. "What?"

"Never mind," I said. "I'll pick one." Grabbing the kettle, I then flipped on the faucet. As I did, I noticed two wineglasses on the dish rack next to the sink. They'd been rinsed, but on the rim of one a faint smear of lipstick remained. I filled the kettle and set it on the burner. While I waited for the water to come to a boil, Nigel returned with one of the paramedics. He was a burly man, with a nose that looked as if it had been broken one too many times and black hair that was pulled back into a tight ponytail. He crossed over to where Harper sat and knelt down in front of her.

"Mrs. Trados?" he asked, his voice gentle. "My name is Steven. I'm just going to check and see how you're doing, if that's okay?"

Harper raised her eyes to his and nodded dumbly. After giving her a reassuring smile, Steven placed a wool blanket around her shoulders and began to check her vitals. As Steven made various reassuring sounds, I made Harper's tea, adding several spoonfuls of sugar and a dollop of cream. Hand-ing her the mug, I said, "Here, Harper, drink this."

Harper looked down at her hands as if surprised to find them holding the mug. "Tea?" she repeated.

"Yes, honey. It's tea. Why don't you take a sip," I said quietly. I glanced up at Nigel. His eyebrows were pulled together in worry. Skippy moved to sit next to me. He gently laid his head in Harper's lap.

"Dan hates tea," Harper said, staring at the mug.

"Your friend is right," Steven chimed in. "A hot cup of tea can help with shock."

Harper raised her eyes to his. "No. Dan hates tea," she repeated stubbornly.

"That's okay," he said in a practiced soothing tone. "Not everyone is a tea person."

Harper suddenly slammed the mug down on the table. "He didn't want me here," she said, glaring at the mug. "I've never been here."

Steven glanced at me, his broad face serious. "I think it might be best if we take her to the hospital for observation," he said in a low voice.

I stared at Harper a beat and then said, "I'm not sure that's going to be necessary. I think what she's saying is that, why is there tea here? For that matter, why are there *several* kinds of tea here? If they weren't for Dan, who were they for?"

When Harper looked up at me, I saw that some of her color had returned. "Exactly," she said. "That's *exactly* what I want to know."

Sixteen

"Who's what for?" Marcy asked as she and Brian rejoined us.

"The tea," I answered.

Marcy raised an eyebrow. "You want to try that again?" she asked.

"Sorry. According to Harper, Dan hated tea," I explained, "but there's tea here."

Brian continued to stare at me. "Lots of tea," I added. Brian still stared. "Dan didn't drink tea," I finally said.

Marcy's eyes widened slightly. "Oh. I see," she said. From Brian's expression, I gathered he did not.

Harper set the offending mug on the kitchen table and pushed it away from her. She pulled the blanket closer around her shoulders and muttered something that sounded suspiciously like *cheating rat bastard.* Perhaps because that's exactly what she muttered. Skippy shoved his head farther into her lap until Harper registered his presence. Staring down at him with an expression of mild surprise, she began to mechanically stroke his massive fawn-colored head.

A woman suddenly exited Dan's bedroom, and all eyes turned to her. It was Deborah Simms, the medical examiner. It had been a few years since I'd last seen her, but she hadn't changed a bit. A no-nonsense woman with jet-black hair and gray eyes, she wore her usual outfit of a black turtleneck and black trousers. Her only concession to color was her trademark slash of ruby-red lipstick. Seeing me, she gave a friendly nod just as an officer rolled the gurney with Dan's body out from the bedroom.

"Nic," she said, as she briskly crossed the room to where I stood. "What are you doing here? I heard you married some gorgeous playboy and moved to LA. Don't tell me you're back on the force?"

I shook my head. "No, I'm actually an old friend of the victim's wife. She called me when she found the body."

Deborah nodded and then her gaze landed on Nigel. "So that makes you . . . ?" she began.

Nigel smiled and stepped forward. "The gorgeous playboy," he said with a wink, "but you can call me Nigel if you prefer."

A faint blush crept up Deborah's neck, and something that sounded suspiciously like a giggle escaped her lips. I glanced at Marcy in surprise. I had never heard Deborah laugh let alone giggle. From the expression on Marcy's face, she seemed as stunned as I was. "It's a pleasure to meet you," Deborah now said, extending her hand.

"And you as well," Nigel said. "Nic always spoke very highly of you."

I forced myself not to roll my eyes at Nigel's obvious attempt at flattery. I had never once mentioned Deborah Simms to him, and he damn well knew it. But if it resulted in getting some information about Dan's death, I wasn't going to argue the point.

Deborah smiled up at him. "So you knew the victim?" she asked.

Nigel nodded. I noticed he was still holding her hand. "We did. We actually saw him just last night. I can't believe that he's dead. It's all so sudden. Do you have any idea what happened? Was it a heart attack?"

Deborah shook her head. "It's too early to tell, of course. I still have to run some tests, but at this point I'm leaning toward poisoning."

"Poison," Marcy repeated.

Deborah shifted her gaze to Marcy and

nodded. "Looks that way. I'll know more once I finish up."

"Could it have been intentional?" Brian now asked.

Deborah raised an eyebrow. "Oh, it was definitely intentional," she said. "But whether it was the victim's intent or someone else's intent I can't answer to yet." Her gaze then landed on Harper, who was still numbly petting Skippy's head. "Is that the victim's wife?" she asked.

"Yes," I answered.

Deborah paused a moment and then asked, "Why does she have a pony with her?"

I swallowed a laugh and explained. "Oh, that's just our dog, Skippy. He's a Bullmastiff."

Deborah looked at me and then at Nigel. "Oh. Someone said something about you and an enormous dog, but I thought they were kidding."

Nigel winked at her again. "No, the stories about Skippy are all true. It's the ones about the pony you need to ignore."

SEVENTEEN

After Deborah left, I turned to Marcy. "What do you think?"

She shook her head. "Nic, you know I can't get into this with you right now."

I smiled and shrugged. "Sorry. Old habits die hard, I guess. Speaking of which, did you notice the wineglasses by the sink? They've been rinsed, but not very well. Looks like there's some lipstick on one of them."

Marcy glanced over toward the sink. "Brian?" she said. "You want to bag those glasses for me?"

Brian nodded and went in search of an evidence bag. Once he'd bagged the glasses, he went outside to give them to the Forensics team.

"Any chance I can take a look at the bedroom?" I asked. "I won't touch a thing. I promise."

Marcy sighed. "Fine. But be quick. Brian

is going to give me hell for you being here as it is."

I nodded my thanks and headed for the bedroom. Nigel trailed behind me. Marcy stood in the doorway and watched us, her arms crossed against her chest. There was a queen bed in the center of the far wall flanked by twin nightstands. The sheets were rumpled and the black comforter hung off to one side. A medium-size chest of drawers was pushed up against the right wall. Pushed against the left wall was a desk, a laptop computer, and small filing cabinet. To the left of the manuscript sat a glass decanter. Nigel walked over to it and eyed the amber fluid curiously. "Can I open this?" he asked Marcy after a minute.

"Nigel, I get that you enjoy your scotch and all, but really?" Marcy replied, her nose wrinkling in annoyance.

Nigel rolled his eyes. "I don't want to drink it, Marcy. I just want to smell it." He glanced back at the decanter.

"Why, what's wrong with it?" I asked.

Nigel tilted his head. "I don't know. The color is off or something. It doesn't look right."

"Well, you would certainly know," I said to Nigel as I shot Marcy a questioning look.

Marcy uncrossed her arms and crossed

over to the desk. Slipping on a pair of blue latex gloves, she gingerly lifted up the glass topper. Nigel moved his head down toward the now open decanter but Marcy held up a hand to stop him. "Ladies first, if you don't mind, Nigel. Or rather, detectives first," she said. Bringing her nose up close to the opening, Marcy closed her eyes and inhaled deeply. After a moment she inhaled again. She opened her eyes and peered at the liquid and then glanced up at Nigel. "I don't smell anything odd," she admitted, "but then, I don't drink the stuff."

She stood up and moved away from the desk, waving Nigel in to her vacated spot as she did. Leaning over the decanter, Nigel briefly inhaled. His nose twitched in distaste and stood up quickly.

"Well?" Marcy asked.

"It's not right," Nigel said, staring down at the liquid.

Marcy raised an eyebrow. "And you can tell that just by sniffing it?"

Nigel tilted his head and shot her a level look. "Is that a serious question?" he asked.

"Right," she acknowledged with a small sigh. "Of course you can."

"Marcy? Are you in here?" Brian suddenly called out from the other room. A second later his dark head popped into view from around the doorjamb. His eyebrows drew together in obvious irritation at the sight of Nigel and me in the bedroom. "What the hell are they doing in here, Marcy?" he barked at her. "Jesus. The Captain will have our asses if he finds out about this."

"He won't if it helps us solve this case faster," Marcy said. "I can't imagine that he's going to enjoy the press's reaction to the probable murder of a well-known theater critic. The sooner we solve this, the better it will be for everyone."

"Meaning what exactly?" Brian asked.

"Meaning that I want this decanter taken in for testing," Marcy answered. "I have it on good authority that there's something off with the scotch."

Brian looked from Marcy to Nigel. Nigel winked. "Make that *very* good authority," he said.

EIGHTEEN

Once Marcy and Brian finished their interview with Harper, Nigel and I insisted on seeing her home. We were all quiet on the ride back to her apartment, mainly because it's hard to chat while a one-hundred-plus-pound bullmastiff is stretched across your lap. We had just stepped into the large foyer when a male voice from the other room called out, "Harpo? Is that you?"

I looked over at Harper in surprise just as a man I guessed to be in his mid-twenties came around the corner. He was about six feet tall with broad shoulders and an athletic build. The dark brown hair on his head was thick and wavy; on his chiseled jawline was fine stubble. The only aspect of his appearance that didn't suggest an ad in a men's fitness magazine was the sleepy baby cradled in his arms. With her tuft of flaxen hair and large green eyes, it was clear that Gracie took after her mother.

The man pulled up short when he saw us, his face pinched with embarrassment. "Oh, I'm sorry," he said to Harper. "I didn't realize you had company."

Harper waved away his apology. "It's fine, Devin," she said. "These are my friends I was telling you about, Nic and Nigel Martini. And, of course, their dog, Skippy." Turning back to us, she added, "This is Devin Fitzgerald. He's Gracie's nanny."

Adroitly shifting Gracie to his left arm, Devin smiled and politely shook our hands. Refusing to be left out of the introductions, Skippy held out his paw as well. Devin gamely shook it too without comment.

"I was just about to put Gracie down for her nap," Devin said to Harper. "I wasn't sure if you wanted me to stay, so I prepped all her bottles for later."

Harper smiled gratefully at him. Walking over to him, she scooped Gracie from his arms and snuggled her close. Gracie mewed and nestled her head into Harper's neck. After a moment Harper said to Devin, "Would you mind terribly staying? I don't know what more the police are going to want from me, and I would feel much better knowing she was with you."

Devin nodded immediately. "Of course I'll stay. I'm happy to help. And again, I'm so sorry for . . . everything," he said his eyes trained on her face. Lowering his voice, he asked, "Do the police have any idea what happened?"

Harper shook her head and buried her face into Gracie's little body. "No, not yet," came her muffled reply.

Devin started to respond when Gracie let out a tired cry. "I know that cry," he said. "I probably should put her down for her nap." Harper kissed Gracie's cheek and handed her to Devin. He snuggled the little girl close, murmuring, "Come on, princess. Time for bed."

After blowing Gracie one last kiss, Harper led us into the living room. It was a comfortable room decorated in shades of cream and fawn, with overstuffed club chairs and a sectional couch. Books spilled haphazardly from a floor-to-ceiling bookcase; several more were stacked on a nearby mahogany writing desk. The walls were adorned with framed theater posters, many of which were signed by the cast.

As soon as Nigel and I were seated on the suede couch, I shot Harper a look. "So *Harpo,* anything you want to share about your nanny?" I asked.

Harper flushed but pretended not to understand my question. "Devin? He's been a godsend. He's so good with Gracie. He absolutely adores her."

"I don't think she's the only one he adores, Harper," I said. "And I don't think I'm going to be the only one who picks up on that."

Harper flushed even more. "Don't be silly, Nic. Devin and I are close, yes, but that's only because he's been helping me with Gracie. For God's sake, he seems fonder of her than her own father was."

"Yes, I caught that," I said.

Harper furrowed her eyebrows and leaned forward. "What's that supposed to mean?"

I took a deep breath and blew it out. "Harper, I'm on your side here, okay? But I know how the police are going to look at this — at least initially. The spouse is always a suspect in a homicide. It's just how it is."

Harper's eyes opened wide and she leaned back. "Homicide? You think Dan was . . . murdered? On purpose?"

"That's usually how it's done," Nigel said not unkindly.

"But . . . but why do you think it was murder?" she asked.

"Call it a hunch. Dan was young and in good health, right?" I asked. Harper gave a cautious nod. "Well, in my experience, men his age don't usually drop dead from natural

116

causes."

"But why would someone kill Dan?" Harper asked. "I mean, he could be difficult, but murder? It doesn't make sense to me."

I shrugged. "I don't know. He did piss off some people with his review last night."

Harper shook her head. "But he does that practically every night — I mean, with his reviews," she added quickly.

I nodded. "I don't doubt that. Maybe someone read one bad review too many and snapped. Or maybe it had nothing to do with his reviews."

Harper's mouth pulled down into a frown. "Meaning?"

"Meaning that it might have something to do with why Dan's apartment was stocked with tea," I said gently.

Harper sat very still for a moment and stared at the flower arrangement on the marble coffee table. "You think he was cheating on me?" she asked in a small voice after a moment.

"I don't know, honey," I said honestly. "What do *you* think?"

Harper stared at her hands and then said, "I think he was a complete and utter bastard."

"That is a sentiment that I completely agree with," said Nigel as he leaned over and gently squeezed her hand, "but one that I think would be best left unshared with the police."

"Speaking of potential conversations with the police," I said, "I image they're going to want to know your whereabouts last night."

Harper's head swung towards me, her mouth open in surprise. "I was here with Gracie."

"Just Gracie?" I asked.

Harper opened her mouth and then shut it, her lips pressed together tightly. After a second, she nodded and said stiffly, "Yes, of course, just with Gracie." When I didn't respond right away, she asked, "Why? Is that a problem?"

"I don't know," I answered honestly. "I wish someone else could testify that you were here all night."

"What are you suggesting, Nic?" Harper asked. "That I lugged my six-month-old daughter out in the middle of the night so I could murder my husband? That's insane!"

I stared at Harper a beat. "No, Harper," I said. "It never occurred to me that you would do such a thing, and if I were you, I would also add that to the list of items you shouldn't share with the police."

"Well, I certainly wouldn't leave her alone!" Harper continued a bit hysterically.

I leaned forward a bit in my chair and took Harper's hand. "Harper, I don't believe anyone is going to think you left Gracie here alone. But I am afraid that the police might wonder if you left her with someone *else.*" I glanced meaningfully down the hallway where Devin had just disappeared.

Harper sucked in her breath. "I don't think I like where you're going with this, Nic."

I sat back against the couch and spread out my hands. "Look, Harper. I know you. I know you didn't kill Dan, but I'm not with the department anymore, okay? And I can tell you that if I didn't know you, you'd be a strong suspect. You were unhappy in your marriage. You wanted a divorce but were worried about the lack of a prenup. Your husband was — apparently — entertaining someone at his apartment on a regular basis. And then there's the little matter of the fact that your nanny seems to be smitten with you. A nanny, I might add, who looks like he's stepped off the cover of *GQ.* Hell, if all nannies looked like him, there'd be a population explosion in this country."

Nigel crossed his leg and smoothed a non-existent wrinkle on his pants. "That's all right," he said, "just pretend I'm not here."

Harper and I did.

"My point is," I continued, "that you are going to be a suspect, and you have no alibi."

"But that's not my fault," Harper protested. "How was I to know that Dan was going to die? He stayed at that damn 'work apartment' more nights than not. Nothing ever happened before!"

"I know, but last night it did," I said. "And, like it or not, that might be a problem for you."

Devin suddenly appeared in the doorway. He glanced nervously at Harper and then to me. "I couldn't help overhear what you were saying," he said quietly. "It won't be a problem."

"What won't be a problem, Devin?" I asked, not knowing if I really wanted to hear the answer.

"About Harpo — I mean Mrs. Trados — needing an alibi." Devin stole another glance at Harper. She was looking up at him with wide eyes and silently shaking her head. "I was here last night," Devin continued. He paused and then added, "*All* night. And Mrs. Trados never left the apartment."

"What?" Harper and I asked at the same time.

Devin walked over to Harper. He placed his hand on her shoulder and gave it a meaningful squeeze. "I know you didn't want to involve me," he said to her slowly as if he was cueing her for her next line, "but we have to tell the truth."

I arched an eyebrow. "And the truth is that you spent the night here?" I asked not trying to hide my doubt.

Devin turned to me and met my gaze. "Yes," he said.

"Why?" I asked.

"Gracie is teething," he answered smoothly. "It's been hard on Har . . . Mrs. Trados, and I offered to stay so she could get some sleep."

"I see. Well, you certainly are dedicated to your *job,*" I said.

Devin ducked his head. "Nothing . . . untoward happened. I just wanted to help. Mr. Trados wasn't a very . . . a very hands-on father, and I could see that Mrs. Trados needed a break. Teething is a hard stage."

"Okay, first of all, no one says *untoward* anymore," I said. "You might want to keep that in mind when you give your statement to the police. You sound like you just stepped out of a BBC period piece." I looked at Harper. She wouldn't meet my eye; instead she stared up at Devin. "Well, Harper?" I asked. "Is this true?"

Harper said nothing for a beat as she and Devin shared some wordless exchange. Finally, she swallowed and turned back to me. "Yes, it's true. Devin offered to stay last night, and I was so tired that I took him up on his offer. We were both here. All night."

She didn't meet my eye as she said this and I wondered which I wanted to believe more — that Devin had spent the night or that he hadn't.

Nineteen

Soon after Devin's announcement, Harper claimed the onset of a sudden headache. After excusing herself to go lie down, Nigel and I said our goodbyes to Devin and left as well. Standing on the sidewalk outside of Harper's apartment and blinking up at the bright afternoon sun, I shook my head in frustration.

"You look like I could use a drink," Nigel said.

"I get that a lot," I replied.

"Let's go to that place on Fifth," he suggested. "The one that Skippy likes."

"And which one is that again?" I asked.

"I forget the name, but they serve those really good Bloody Marys."

"Oh, yes. I know the one you're talking about," I said. "However, I didn't realize Skippy had developed such a discerning pallet for specialty drinks, especially as most days he prefers to drink out of the toilet."

Nigel shrugged. "I've been trying to broaden his horizons. Right now, he just likes to eat the olives, but I have every confidence that he'll graduate to celery soon."

"You're a regular Henry Higgins."

Nigel winked. "Hey, look at what I did with *you.*"

My phone began to ring just then, sparing Nigel a well-deserved smack to the back of his head. I glanced down at the screen; it was Peggy. I showed the readout to Nigel. "Why don't you take the call over there," Nigel said, pointing to a nearby bench. "I'll see if I can't find us some coffee."

I nodded and sat down before answering the phone. "Hey, Peggy," I said.

"Nic," Peggy began in her typical breathless fashion. "Jesus, what a day it's been! The matinee just got out, and I think everything went fine, but it was touch-and-go there for a moment. Guess, what happened?"

"Actually, I . . ."

"Oh, never mind. You'll never guess, so I'll just tell you. Nina never showed up this morning! Can you believe it? Just did not show up! I mean, her understudy was happy to step in, and Molly's great and all, but I couldn't believe it. I finally got ahold of

124

Nina and do you know what she said?"

"Peg, I need to . . ."

"She was all apologies, saying how she'd been throwing up all night with some stomach bug, but if you ask me she didn't show because she was still upset about Dan's review. Not that I blame her, of course. What he said was pretty rotten, but still!"

I tried again. "Peg, about Dan —"

"Oh, I know," said Peggy. "I shouldn't have called him a jerk in front of Harper. I actually wanted to call him far worse than that, but I doubt that will count in my favor as an apology. But I was just so mad. I swear, sometimes I want to kill him."

"Yeah, you *really* shouldn't say that," I began, but Peggy kept going.

"I know, I know," she said with a huff. "You don't need to say it. Evan already gave me the lecture. Don't worry. I plan on apologizing to her right away. I just hope Dan didn't hear me. That man can hold a grudge"

"I don't think that's going to be an issue," I said.

"What about Harper?" Peggy asked. "I've been trying to call her all morning, but she's not answering her phone. I guess she's pretty mad at me, huh?"

"Peggy. Harper is not mad at you, and Dan is definitely not mad at you. The only person who is getting mad at you is *me.*"

"You? Why? What did I do to you?" she asked.

"You keep interrupting me. Now please shut up for two minutes. I need to tell you something," I said.

"Ok. Ok," Peggy huffed. "You don't need to tell me twice."

I took a deep breath and resisted the urge to debate that dubious point. "I have some bad news. Apparently, Dan stayed at his apartment last night and never came home. Harper went over there this morning and found him —"

With an audible gasp, Peggy interrupted again. "Oh my God!" she exclaimed. "Did she find him in bed with another woman? I always thought Dan was an ass, but I never thought he'd cheat on her. God, what a pig. I'm so glad I didn't apologize to him."

"Uh, not exactly, Peg," I said. "Harper found him in bed, all right. But he wasn't with another woman."

"He wasn't with another *man,* was he?" Peggy asked, aghast.

"Peg! Will you let me finish? He wasn't with *anyone.* He was dead."

Peggy was silent. Then she said, "I swear

126

to God, Nic, if this is your idea of a joke . . .”

I closed my eyes. “Yeah, Peg,” I said, not bothering to hide my sarcasm. “It’s all a big gag. Pretty funny, huh?” Nigel returned and placed a cup of hot coffee in my free hand. I smiled at him and took a grateful sip.

“Shit, Nic. Really?” said Peggy. “Dan is dead? Oh dear God. Poor Harper! What . . . what happened?”

“I don’t know really. At first Harper thought that he’d had a heart attack, but I’m not so sure that’s the case.”

“Meaning what exactly?” Peggy asked slowly.

“Meaning I don’t think Dan died of natural causes,” I answered.

There was a long pause before Peggy said anything. “And what do you think he died from?” she finally asked.

“That I don’t know,” I admitted. “The police suspect he was poisoned.”

“Poisoned! You’re serious, aren’t you? But why would someone poison Dan? I mean, I get that the man is . . . well, *was* an ass, but so are lots of people!”

“And lots of people get murdered,” I pointed out.

Peggy fell quite again. After a moment, she said, “How’s Harper doing?”

“She’s as good as can be expected,” I said.

"She's lying down now."

"Oh. Is Devin with her?"

"Probably," I said. "But I didn't stay long enough to tuck them in."

"Huh?" Peggy said. "I meant, is Devin there to help with Gracie? What the hell did *you* mean?"

"Just that Devin is apparently infatuated with Harper — or as he calls her, *Harpo* — and spent last night with her."

Peggy's reaction to this was inarticulate sputtering.

"Apparently Gracie is teething," I added, as if that clarified the situation.

The sputtering stopped. "Are you messing with me now?" Peggy demanded.

"Sadly, I am not," I admitted.

"Teething? Gracie is *teething*?" Peggy repeated. "What does that even mean? Is that some kind of new slang?"

"I don't think so. But it's the reason Devin gave for spending the night. The thing is, I'm not even sure I believe he did spend the night. It's clear he has feelings for Harper, but I don't know if he's saying he spent the night to give Harper an alibi or because he really spent the night."

"I seriously think my brain is going to explode. I need a drink. Where are you?"

"Nigel and I were about to go get a drink

at that place on Fifth that serves the really good Bloodys," I answered.

"Martin's?"

"That's the one," I said.

"Well, why don't you come here first and then we can all head over together. Evan is already here. I just have to go over a few notes with the cast. Oh!" she paused as if struck by a thought. "Do you think I should tell them? About Dan, I mean?"

I took a sip of my coffee and considered her question. "Actually, do you mind holding off on telling them until I get there? I'm curious to see how they react."

"Jesus, Nic. You don't really think one of them could have had anything to do with it, do you?"

"I honestly don't know, Peg." Silence answered. "Peg? You still there?"

"Yeah. I'm here." She paused a moment. "He's really dead?" she asked.

"He's really dead," I said.

"Well, shit."

"Yeah, that about sums it up," I agreed.

TWENTY

Twenty minutes later, we were still vainly searching for a taxi. It wasn't that there weren't any available; there were. Plenty, in fact. It was just that none seemed to be in the mood to transport a large dog, or as one particularly loquacious cabbie put it "some half-bred transient Yeti." Finally, Nigel left Skippy and me on a nearby bench while he went in search of a driver amenable to bribery. Ten minutes later, I was thumbing through some emails on my phone when I heard Nigel call my name. I looked up expecting to see a familiar pair of blue eyes. What I saw, however, while ocular in nature, was neither blue nor a pair. Instead, a single brown orb gazed placidly down at me. I reached out to gently pat the smooth fur of the horse's muzzle before angling my head until I could see Nigel. He grinned at me from the confines of a bright red gig.

"We're taking a horse drawn carriage?" I

130

asked rather unnecessarily.

Nigel alighted with an agile jump and kissed the back of my hand with exaggerated flourish. "We are indeed, my fair lady," he said. Gesturing to the bored young man seated on the padded bench, he added, "This gallant young squire, who also answers to the name of Toby, has agreed to ferry us to our desired location in exchange for a sack of gold coin."

From his seat, Toby let out a sigh. "Look, buddy. I said I'd take you, but it's fifty bucks. Cash or credit *only.*"

Nigel pulled me up from my bench and helped me into the carriage. Skippy jumped up behind me and settled into the seat next to Nigel. Nigel slung his arm around him. "You know," I said, as I watched, "when I thought about taking a horse drawn carriage with you through New York, this isn't exactly what I envisioned."

"I know what you mean," Nigel agreed. "It's not how I imagined it either."

I paused a moment and then asked, "It's because you saw yourself wearing a top hat, isn't it?"

Nigel looked at me in surprise. "Why? You didn't?"

TWENTY-ONE

We arrived in due time at the theater. It took several minutes longer than necessary to alight from the carriage as we were stopped by several tourists who thought Skippy was one of the horses from *Equus*. Nigel saw no reason to dissuade them of this and offered to pose for pictures.

By the time we made our way into the theater, Peggy was just finishing her post-play review with the cast. Mark was sitting on a bench next to Brooke, who was taking notes in a thick leather-bound journal. Jeremy stood off to one side, leaning against a doorjamb, surreptitiously checking his phone. In spite of his stage makeup, his complexion was haggard. A woman I didn't recognize stood next to him. Based on her blond wig and costume, I guessed that she was Nina's understudy, Molly.

Hearing our entrance, Peggy looked back and waved us over. As we approached, her gaze dropped to Skippy; seconds later, her jaw followed suit. "Dear God, is that a dog?" she asked.

Nigel put his fingers over his lips. "Yes," he said in a hushed voice, "but we haven't told him yet. We're waiting until he's older."

Peggy rolled her eyes as she scratched Skippy's ears. "Well, speaking of telling people unpleasant truths, I haven't told the cast about Dan yet," she said in a low voice. "Do you think I should do it now?"

"Might as well," I said. "The press is bound to find out sooner rather than later."

Peggy nodded at me and then raised her voice to the cast. "One last thing, everyone," she said. "I'm afraid I have a bit of bad news to share." All eyes focused on Peggy. I tried to gauge everyone's expression as Peggy made the announcement. "Dan Trados died last night."

Brooke let out a little gasp and covered her mouth with her hand. Her journal slipped off her lap and fell to the floor. Mark immediately leaned over and picked it up. He handed it back to her and wrapped a comforting arm around her shoulders. Jeremy blinked several times but said nothing. Nina's understudy, Molly, glanced around at the others before saying, "He's that theater critic with *Vanity Fair,* right?"

She was made up to look like a woman in her late fifties, but based on her voice and movements, I guessed she was far younger.

Peggy nodded. "Yes, Molly. That's him."

Molly's eyes grew wide. "Holy shit. What happened?"

Peggy glanced at me before answering. "It's unclear," she said. "The police haven't said —"

"The police!" Brooke cried out, the journal once again sliding out of her hands and landing on the floor with a thud. This time, Mark did not retrieve it. "Why are the police involved?" she asked.

"Well," began Peggy, "it seems that . . . well, *apparently* . . ." She stopped and looked helplessly at me.

"The police haven't determined how Mr. Trados died yet," I said, taking a step forward.

Mark looked over at me, his gaze wary. "But the police are involved," he said slowly. "Meaning that . . ." He paused and glanced at Brooke. Brooke's posture was rigid; her gaze riveted to the stage floor.

"Meaning that the police suspect foul play," I finished.

Molly suddenly let out a low whistle. "Holy shit," she said. "Does Nina know?"

"I don't know," I answered. "Why do you ask?"

Molly's eyes narrowed as she studied me. "I'm sorry, but who are you?" she asked.

"Nic Martini," I answered. "I went to school with Peggy and Harper Trados. Why did you ask about Nina?"

Molly paused and seemed to consider her answer. "Oh, no reason, really. I mean, it's just that she was pretty angry with him last night. About that review he wrote . . . and everything." She stopped and blinked. "I mean, I would have been, too . . . I didn't mean to imply . . . I just wondered if . . ." Molly paused again and took a deep breath. "You know what? I'm just going to stop talking now."

Next to her, Jeremy rolled his eyes. "You think?" he muttered. Molly's cheeks flushed crimson and she stared at her feet.

"I don't know what Nina knows," Peggy said. "Obviously, she didn't say anything to me about it when she called me this morning." Turning to me, Peggy asked, "Did you want to say anything else?"

I shook my head. "No. I imagine the police will get in touch with everyone themselves."

Brooke gave a startled shudder. "Why would the police want to talk to any of us?"

she asked. "What could we possibly have to do with Dan's death? Are you saying that we are somehow suspects?"

I tried to smile reassuringly, but based on the panic in Brooke's wide eyes, it wasn't working. "I'm not saying any such thing," I said. "I just happen to know the detective in charge of the case. Actually, she's my old partner. And Detective Garcia is very thorough. I expect she'll want to talk with everyone who had any kind of interaction with Dan last night."

Jeremy stared at me with an expression of mild horror. "Wait. You're a detective?" he sputtered.

"Ex-detective," I clarified.

Based on the way Jeremy suddenly went pale and abruptly sat down in a nearby chair, the distinction did not seem to mollify him.

TWENTY-TWO

"So do you really think Dan was having an affair?" Peggy asked me as she took a sip of her Bloody Mary sometime later. We were seated at an outdoor patio table at Martin's. Skippy lay under the table. Sprawled on his back with his paws in the air, he was softly snoring.

"I don't know," I said. "I *did* find two empty wineglasses at his apartment, one of which had lipstick on it. It can't have been from Harper. She's never even been to his apartment."

Peggy shook her head. "That bastard."

"Poor Harper," said Evan as he took a sip from his own drink. "None of us can pretend that we liked Dan, but this isn't how I wanted to see him exit Harper's life."

"I disagree," Peggy said firmly. "I actually think it's better off this way."

Evan paused mid-sip to stare at his wife in horror. "It's better off what way? With

Dan *dead*? Are you actually saying it's better that he's *dead*?"

"Well, not for Dan, of course," Peggy said. "I imagine he'd prefer things ended differently. I was thinking more of Harper."

Evan continued to gape at his wife. "How on earth is Dan dying better for Harper?" he asked.

"Well, for one thing," said Peggy, "she doesn't have to deal with a messy divorce now."

Evan set his drink down with a thud. "Oh, that's right. Instead, she gets to plan a funeral," he said his voice dripping with sarcasm. "What was I thinking? That's a *much* better option."

Peggy rolled her eyes. "You know what I mean."

"No, I don't think I do," Evan said. "Are you saying that if I was cheating on you, you'd rather I turn up dead?"

"Of course not," Peggy said reassuringly. "If you were cheating on me, I wouldn't hope for you to turn up dead."

"Well, that's good to know," Evan said, somewhat mollified. He picked up his drink again.

"You didn't let me finish," said Peggy, holding up her hand. "A, you would never cheat on me but, B, if you did, I wouldn't *hope* for you to turn up dead, because you *would* turn up dead. By me."

Evan shook his head. "*This* is the kind of stuff that should have come out during all those premarital classes we had to take with your church. Instead of focusing on who would be in charge of finances, maybe we should have discussed your views on manslaughter."

Peggy tilted her head and stared at Evan with a challenging smile. "Why? Are you saying you would have done things differently?"

Evan took a sip of his drink. "I might have opted for a less generous life-insurance plan for myself," he muttered.

Peggy laughed and tapped him on his nose. "Oh, please. The mere fact that I'd kill you if you cheated on me is only proof of how much I love you."

Evan laughed as she blew him a kiss and took another sip of her drink.

"Too bad you're already married," I said as our waitress reached our table with a fresh round of drinks. "That would have made a great addition to the traditional vows."

Nigel dug out an olive from his drink and gave a low whistle before tossing the garnish into the air. Seconds later, Skippy's sleek brown head emerged from under the table. With an agile snap, he caught the treat and then sank back down out of sight.

Peggy blinked at the display. "I feel like I just watched Nessy breach the surface of Loch Ness."

Evan took a sip from his drink. "What happens now?" he asked. "I mean, with the police?"

I shrugged. "They'll wait until they get the report from the coroner about how Dan died and go from there," I said. "If it turns out that he was really murdered, then they'll start looking at motives and begin to interview everyone."

"Do *you* think he was murdered?" Evan asked me.

"My gut tells me he was," I admitted. "Young, relatively healthy guys like Dan generally don't just drop dead. I talked with the coroner, too. She's an old friend and really good at her job. She suspects it was poison."

"So maybe whoever Dan had that drink with might have poisoned him?" Peggy asked.

I took a sip of my drink before answering. "Possibly."

Peggy let out a shaky breath. "Then the police will be looking for a woman."

I shook my head. "The police are going to look at everyone with a motive to kill Dan."

Peggy let out a grim laugh. "That's going to be a long list. Dan wasn't liked very much."

"Yes" I said. "Maybe it's because of my former experience with law enforcement, but I was able to sniff that one out myself."

Peggy was quiet for a moment and then said, "Harper is going to be a suspect, isn't she?"

I gave a reluctant nod. "Unfortunately, the spouse is usually a suspect in a murder case. And the fact that Harper was unhappy and wanted a divorce isn't going to help her case. And then there's the little problem of Devin."

Peggy leaned forward on the table, her eyes wide with interest. "Yes, what is *that* all about? Do you really think they're having an affair?"

I shrugged. "I honestly don't know. It's clear that Devin has a crush on her, but I don't know how Harper feels. But in any case, Devin overheard me tell Harper that she was most likely going to be a suspect, and he immediately claimed that he spent last night helping her take care of Gracie and that Harper never left."

Peggy considered my answer. "Well, I for

one hope they *are* having an affair. Devin is an absolute sweetheart and is amazing with Gracie. Plus, he's *gorgeous.* He looks like he's just stepped out of an *Abercrombie and Fitch* catalog."

Evan wagged a finger in her face. "Hold on a sec," he said. "Leaving aside the 'gorgeous' comment — which, trust me, we will address later — how is it okay for Harper to have an affair but not Dan?"

Peggy rolled her eyes. "Because, if Harper *was* having an affair it was because Dan drove her to it."

Evan closed his eyes in obvious frustration. "You know you're being a complete and total hypocrite right now, don't you?" he asked.

Next to him, Nigel gently shook his head. "Forget it, man," he said in a low voice. "You are not going to win this argument. Ever."

Peggy ignored them both. "Do you think the police will believe Devin's story?" she asked me.

"I don't know," I said. "They could assume that he's lying to cover for her. She may need more than just his word to prove she wasn't at Dan's apartment."

Peggy fell silent and stared at her drink. With her brow furrowed, she idly traced patterns on the glass's condensation with her finger. "I keep thinking about Nina," she said after a minute. "It's not like her to call in sick. Two years ago she was playing the lead in *Kiss Me, Kate,* and started having terrible stomach pains halfway through the opening night. She not only finished the play but also came back for three curtain calls. An hour later, she was in surgery for acute appendicitis."

"Are you saying you think she wasn't really sick?" I asked.

Peggy sat back in her chair with a frustrated sigh. "I don't know. The thing is, I really like Nina. She can be unpredictable and a pain in the ass at times, but I like her. I hate the idea of telling the police about her reaction to Dan's review and how she called out sick today. I'd feel like I was throwing Nina under the bus to save Harper."

"I'm sure plenty of other people are going to mention Dan's review and Nina's absence today," I said. "You're not throwing anybody under the bus. And besides, the police aren't going to only focus on one person. They are going to look at anyone and everyone who had a problem with Dan."

Peggy blinked suddenly. "Oh! I just remembered something," she said. "I don't know if it means anything, but at one point last night I happened to overhear Dan arguing with his assistant Zack." She paused. "Well, actually, Zack was arguing with Dan. I didn't catch much of what he was saying, but it seemed like he was trying to convince Dan of something. I could tell that Dan didn't agree with him, because he had that pinched look on his face. You know the one I mean," she clarified, "where he looked like he just caught a whiff of bad cheese."

I nodded. "I do indeed. It was featured prominently during our wedding reception."

Peggy laughed. "Well, in any case, it might make sense to talk with Zack. He might know something."

TWENTY-THREE

Nigel was showing me the finer points of a new technique he'd recently read about when my cell phone rang. Not wanting to interrupt him, I ignored it. However, after the caller rang for a tenth time, I finally answered it. I may have been a tad grumpy in my greeting.

"Nic?" said Marcy. "Are you okay? You sound winded."

"I'm fine," I said as I slapped Nigel's hands away. "I was just in the middle of something. What's up?"

"I just thought I'd let you know that I just got Deborah's report. Dan Trados died from acute poisoning. She says it was arsenic. So we're treating it as a homicide."

"Was it in the decanter?" I asked.

"No, actually, it wasn't. The decanter was clean. Just plain scotch in there. So tell Nigel for me that his famous booze nose must be slipping."

"What about the wineglasses? Did the lab find anything in them?" I asked.

"No," Marcy said. "They were scrubbed clean."

I thought about that for a moment. "They were scrubbed clean?" I repeated. "And yet one still had traces of lipstick on the rim?"

Marcy made a noise of agreement. "Yeah. I wondered about that, too. Either someone was in a hurry . . ."

"Or someone wanted us to think Dan had a female visitor," I finished.

"Exactly," said Marcy. "Anyway, I just thought I'd let you know what we've found out so far." She paused and then said, "And, Nic?"

"Yeah?"

"Just a heads up," she said. "It's not looking too good for your friend, Harper. I thought you should know."

"Why? What happened?" I asked.

"Well, we learned that your friend wanted a divorce. Can't say I blame her. From what we found at the apartment, it seems Mr. Trados was entertaining female guests, or at least he was prepared to."

"I gather we're not talking about the Costco supply of tea, are we?" I asked.

Marcy gave a short laugh. "No. We're talking about a Costco supply of condoms."

146

"Well, that's a horrible image," I said.

"Trust me, it was," Marcy said. "This is strictly off the record, I'd have killed the son-of-a-bitch as well."

"But Marcy, she *didn't* kill him. You don't understand, I *know* Harper."

"Nic, I do understand. But with all due respect, you're biased on this one and it's clouding your judgment. If you didn't know her, are you really telling me that she wouldn't be a suspect? Have you met that piece of eye candy she has for a nanny or manny or whatever the hell you want to call him?"

I sighed. "Yeah, I've met Devin. And I get what you're saying. But the fact is that I do know Harper. And maybe she wanted a divorce, and maybe there is something going on with Devin, but she's not a killer. She's not, Marcy. You just have to believe me."

Marcy was quiet for a moment. "I hear you, Nic, I really do," she finally said. "But Brian is making some noise on this and the higher-ups have taken notice. It's a high-profile case, and there's outside pressure to get it wrapped up fast."

I let out a frustrated sigh. It was never a good thing when the higher-ups got involved. People started rushing to judgment and mistakes were made.

"Have you talked to Nina Durand yet?" I asked.

"No," said Marcy. "But I'm scheduled to talk to her later today."

"Good," I said. "Because Dan was particularly nasty about her in his review. Nina didn't take kindly to it; she slapped him across the face."

"Yes, I heard that."

"Did you also hear that Nina was a no-show for the matinee today?" I asked. "From what I gather, that's highly unusual for her. She's not known to call out sick."

"I know that too, Nic," Marcy said. "Don't worry. I'm not going to rush to judgment. I certainly haven't made up my mind. I just wanted to let you know what the general consensus around here is. And, unfortunately, it's that your friend is guilty."

I sighed. "Okay, thanks for the heads up, Marcy."

"Sure thing. I'll keep you posted," she said.

"Oh, quick question before you hang up," I said. "Dan was working on a book. It was a compilation of some of his reviews, as well as bits of celebrity gossip. It might prove interesting reading. I was wondering if I could get a copy of it."

148

Now Marcy sighed. "Jesus, Nic. You know I can't do that."

"Well, can I at least take a look at it?" I asked.

There was a long pause and then Marcy said, "I'll see what I can do."

"Thanks, Marcy. I owe you one."

At this Marcy laughed. "You always were lousy with math. You owe me a hell of a lot more than *one,*" she said as she hung up.

Nigel cocked an eyebrow at me. "Well, what's the latest?"

I leaned back against the headboard. "Well, Dan was definitely poisoned. With arsenic. But it wasn't in the decanter of scotch like you thought. Marcy said to tell you that your expert nose is slipping."

Nigel rolled over onto his stomach and flung his arm across my lap. "I never said that the scotch was poisoned," he said. "I just said that something was wrong with it."

"What does that mean?" I asked with a smile as I played with his hair. "Was it a bad year or something?"

"No, although it probably was," he answered. "All I meant was that it wasn't a single malt. It was a blend."

"I don't follow."

Nigel rolled onto his back, his head now on my lap. "Dan only drank single malt scotch; not blends. In fact, he hated blends. I remember because it was one of the few things we had in common."

I blinked down at him. "Lots of people keep liquor in their homes that they might not drink themselves. Maybe he had friends who liked blends."

Nigel shook his head. "Firstly, I highly doubt Dan had friends. Secondly, I can't see him bothering to notice what other people drank, but thirdly, and most importantly, even if he did, he sure as hell wouldn't put a drink he disliked in his *only* decanter."

I stared down into Nigel's blue eyes. "Has anyone ever told you that you're amazing?" I asked.

Nigel's mouth twisted into a suggestive smirk. "If you think that's amazing," he said as he flipped me onto my back, "wait until I finish showing you what I was doing when Marcy called. You're going to think I'm bloody brilliant."

He was right.

TWENTY-FOUR

I called Harper a little while later. Her voice sounded thick and disorientated when she answered. "I didn't wake you, did I?" I asked.

"Oh, no," she said, giving a rueful laugh. "I don't seem to be able to sleep much these days. But when I am awake, I feel like I'm in a horrible dream."

"I know," I said. "The whole thing is a nightmare. How are you doing though? Do you need me to get anything? Do you need help with Gracie?"

"That's sweet of you," Harper said, "but I'm fine. Devin is here, and he's been wonderful." I opted not to ask for details on that statement. "And I finally got hold of my dad. He's been in London on business, but he was able to book a flight home tonight."

"That's good," I said. I felt better knowing Donald would be on hand to help Harper. Not only did he adore her, but he also was one of those people you could count on to stay levelheaded in times of a crisis. And this certainly qualified as one of those times. "By the way, would you happen to have Zack's number?" I asked.

Harper paused. "Zack? Oh, sure. Let me find it. Hang on." A few seconds later, Harper came back on the line. "Nic? I have it right here. Got a pencil?"

I told her I did. I wrote down the number and thanked her.

"Why do you want to talk to Zack?" she asked.

"Oh, I just wanted to ask him some questions," I said, unsure whether Marcy had called Harper yet with the coroner's ruling.

"The police think Dan was murdered," she said, answering my unspoken question.

"I know," I said. "Marcy called me."

"She called me, too," Harper said. "She was . . . very kind."

I winced, thinking how Harper must have reacted to hearing about Dan's stash of condoms. "Ah, I hoped she wasn't going to tell you about that," I said.

"Tell me about what?" Harper asked.

"The condoms," I said, just as I realized I needed to stop talking.

"What condoms?" Harper asked.

I sighed. "The ones they found in Dan's apartment."

"I don't understand," said Harper slowly. "They found condoms in Dan's apartment?"

"I'm sorry, Harper," I said. "I thought Marcy already told you. I never would have said anything otherwise. God knows you've already been through enough."

"I don't believe it," Harper said.

"I know, honey. The whole thing is just hellish," I said.

"No, I mean I don't believe Dan had condoms there," Harper said.

"I'm not sure I'm following you," I said. "I don't think the police planted them there, if that's what you're saying."

"What kind were they?" Harper suddenly asked.

I paused. "Seriously?" I said. "You want to know what *kind* they were?"

"Yes," Harper said.

"Okay. Why?"

"Because Dan was allergic to latex," she said. "He hated using condoms, even the ones that were latex-free."

"He was allergic?" I asked. "Really?"

"Yes," Harper said.

Something in her tone gave me pause. "Will his doctor testify to that?"

Now Harper paused. "Well, he wasn't allergic so much as he was sensitive to it."

I closed my eyes and sighed. "Harper . . ." I began, but she cut me off.

"No, Nic. Listen to me. I know that Dan could be a real jerk at times, and I realize that I probably sound like the classic wife who's in denial. I mean, he got a 'work apartment' and stocked it with tea, which he didn't drink, but I just don't believe he kept condoms there. Something is not right. But call Zack. He and Dan were working a lot on Dan's book and spending lots of time together. He might know something I don't."

I was quiet a moment. Harper whispered something to someone on her end. A male voice whispered back.

"Okay, Harper. I'll call Zack and Marcy and see what I can find out."

Harper sighed. "Thanks, Nic."

I hung up. I really hoped that Marcy hadn't heard the same male voice when she spoke to Harper earlier. It might give her the wrong idea. I know it certainly gave me the wrong idea.

TWENTY-FIVE

My phone call to Marcy went about how I expected it to go. "I'm sorry," she'd said after a long pause. "You want to know *what*?"

"You heard me," I said. "What kind were they?"

"Are you doing research or something?"

"No, Harper said that Dan was allergic to latex," I said.

"Allergic," she repeated doubtfully.

"Or at least, sensitive to it," I amended.

Marcy tried to hide her bark of laughter. She failed. "I'm sorry, Nic. I didn't mean to laugh, but if I had a dollar for every time a guy told some girl he couldn't wear protection because he had a latex allergy, I could buy a house in your neighborhood."

I sighed. "I know it sounds stupid, Marcy. Believe me. I know. But I promised Harper that I would ask you."

"Okay, fine. Hang on one second and I'll

see if it's in the report."

"Thanks, Marcy," I said. "I owe —"

"Yeah, yeah," Marcy said. "Save it." A second later, she put me on hold. Easy listening music filled my ears.

I was belting out the lyrics to "All By Myself," when Marcy came back on the line. "You want me to put you back on hold so you can finish?" Marcy asked.

"No, I'm good," I said.

"Okay. But don't say I didn't ask," Marcy said. "Anyway, according to the report they were Trojans." She paused. "And they were latex. Looks like I just got another imaginary dollar."

I laughed. "I'll call our real estate agent and tell her to keep an eye out for a house near us."

"You do that," said Marcy. "Did you need anything else, or can I get back to work?"

"Well, since you mentioned it, I'd love to get a copy of the coroner's report," I said.

Marcy let out another bark of laughter just before the line went dead. Either that or she hung up on me.

It was probably the latter.

TWENTY-SIX

My next call was to Zack. He seemed surprised to hear from me. Either that or he'd developed a stutter since I last spoke with him. "Hello, Mrs. Martini," he said. "What can I do for you?"

"I hope I'm not bothering you, Zack, but I wanted to talk to you about Dan."

There was a pause, and then Zack said, "Oh, sure. What do you want to know?"

"Well, this really isn't a conversation I want to have over the phone," I said. "It seems that Dan's death was no accident."

"I don't understand," Zack sputtered. "What do you mean it wasn't an accident?"

"It means he was killed, Zack."

"Right. Of course it does. Sorry," he said. "Jesus. Someone killed him? God, that's awful. I mean, I know he got under people's skin from time to time, but . . . wow." He paused again. "But why do you want to talk to me? You can't think *I* had anything to do

157

with it, do you?" His voice cracked. "Oh God! This is about the magazine asking me to take over Dan's column, isn't it? I swear to you I didn't know that was going to happen! I swear!"

"No one is accusing you of anything, Zack," I said with more patience than I felt. "I just want to talk to you. After all, you worked with Dan. You might be able to shed some light on who would want him dead." This time there was a longer stretch of silence. "Zack?" I finally said. "Are you still there?"

Zack cleared his throat. "Yes, I'm here. Sorry about that." Lowering his voice, he said, "I don't know how much help I can be, but I'll do what I can."

"That's all I'm asking," I said. "I'm staying at the Ritz. Do you think you could meet me at the Star Lounge?"

"Okay. I can do that. I have to get something out first. I could meet you around three, if that works."

"It does. Thank you, Zack. I'll see you at three."

The Star Lounge is mainly known for its head bartender, Norman, his excellent drinks, and as a place to spy a celebrity or two. But my favorite aspect has always been its afternoon tea service. Nigel, Skippy, and I said our hellos to Norman and then secured a table in the cozy wood-paneled room. A petite waitress named Catherine came over and cheerfully took our order for tea.

True to his word, Zack entered the lounge at three o'clock sharp. His steps faltered when he caught sight of Skippy, and he came to a full stop. I couldn't fault him, really. Skippy could be an intimidating sight. Plus, there was the small detail that he was actually sitting in a chair at our table.

"Skippy, get down and let the nice man have a seat," Nigel said.

Skippy did not move.

"Skippy," Nigel repeated in a firmer voice. "We talked about this. Don't make me take away your allowance."

Giving Nigel a baleful look, Skippy vacated the chair. "Good boy," Nigel praised. Skippy ignored him and curled up on the floor next to me. Nigel glanced back up at Zack. "Just ignore him," he said. "He stayed up too late last night watching reruns of *Animal Kingdom* and has been in a mood all day."

Skippy let out an annoyed huff and nestled his head between his paws.

Zack gave a faint nod of his head and

scuttled crab-like into the empty seat. His eyes, however, remained on Skippy.

"Thanks for meeting with us, Zack," I said. "I hope we haven't disrupted your day."

Zack tore his eyes away from Skippy and looked at me from behind his owlish glasses. His face was pale. "Oh, no," he said with a wan smile. "It's fine. I'm glad to help."

"So will you be taking over Dan's position at *Vanity Fair*?" I asked.

Zack swallowed and nodded. "I think so," he said. "I mean, it's not definite yet. But like I said on the phone, Mrs. Martini, I had no idea —"

I held up a hand to stop him. "And like I said on the phone, Zack, I'm not accusing you of anything. I just wanted to talk to you and get an idea of what Dan has been up to recently. Had he upset anyone with a review or pissed anybody off at the magazine lately?"

Zack looked at me with a curious expression and then glanced down at his lap. "Zack?" I prompted.

Zack looked up at me, his expression pained. "I don't mean to sound flip, Mrs. Martini, but Dan pissed people off on a weekly basis."

I nodded at the truth of this. "I see your

point. Well, did you happen to notice any-thing out of the ordinary?"

Zack shook his head. "That's just the thing, I didn't," he said. "Are the police sure he was killed? It couldn't have been, I don't know, an accident?"

"No, they're pretty sure," I said.

"But it's got to be a *mistake* somehow," Zack said running a hand through his hair. "He just became a *dad.* It's not right."

"No, it's not," I agreed.

Zack fell quiet and stared at his lap. "How did it happen?" he asked suddenly.

"Why do you ask?" I said.

Zack flushed. "I don't know. Morbid curiosity, I guess. I'm sorry I asked. It's none of my business."

"He was poisoned," I said after a beat.

Zack waited for me to say more. I didn't. "Well, I don't know how much help I can be," he said. "Dan and I weren't close friends or anything."

"I know, but Harper figured that since you'd been spending so much time together lately that you might have noticed some-thing," I said.

Zack stared at me in confusion. "Why would Harper think I was spending a lot of time with Dan?" he asked.

"She mentioned that the two of you were

spending a lot of late nights working on his book." As soon as I said the words, I realized my mistake. Zack's mouth opened in surprise and then abruptly closed as Catherine returned with our tea. Placing the heavy silver tray on the table, she pointed out the different kinds of sandwiches and desserts before pouring the tea. Once we were served, she pulled a few dog biscuits from her pocket. She placed them on a plate and handed it to Nigel, saying, "In case, Master Skippy is hungry." Hearing his name, Skippy immediately sat up.

"Thank you, Catherine," Nigel said, taking the plate from her. Skippy eyed the plate hungrily.

"My pleasure, Mr. Martini," she said. "Please let me know if I can be of further service."

We promised that we would. As she left, I turned to Nigel. "Why does she know Skippy's name?" I asked.

"Darling, I think it's safe to say that the entire hotel knows Skippy at this point," Nigel said as he handed Zack his cup and saucer.

Skippy placed both of his paws on the armrests of Nigel's chair and stared down at Nigel. Nigel moved the plate with the biscuits out of reach and wagged his finger in Skippy's face. "Don't be greedy, Skippy," he admonished. "You know very well that it's polite to serve our guests first."

Skippy waited until I had my tea before he laid his head in Nigel's lap and whined. Nigel took one of the biscuits and tossed it to him. "There you go. Now, lie down and be a good boy, Skippy," he said. "The grown-ups need to talk."

Skippy obediently flopped back onto the floor. I helped myself to a lobster and caviar tea sandwich while Nigel opted for the egg salad and black truffle. Zack ate nothing. He stared at his tea, his face flushed.

"So Zack" I said after taking a sip of tea, "I gather Dan wasn't burning the midnight oil. Well, not with you anyway."

Zack glanced away before clearing his throat and saying, "Oh, no. We were working together a lot. On the book. Sorry, I wasn't thinking clearly."

I shook my head. "I'm sure you mean well, Zack, but I really don't recommend that you use that lie when the police interview you."

Zack's face flushed red. "What do you mean?" he asked not meeting my eyes.

"It means that Dan told Harper he was spending time working with you — a fact that you apparently were unaware of."

163

Zack let out a sigh. "I'm sorry. It's just that Mrs. Trados seems like such a nice lady. She just lost her husband. It seems cruel to let her find out that Dan was . . ." Zack trailed off.

"Cheating on her?" I finished.

Zack nodded miserably.

"Any idea with whom?" I asked.

Zack shook his head. "As I said, we weren't friends. He was my boss. We didn't really share much about out personal lives." Zack blew out a shaky breath. "But based on snippets of phone conversations I happened to overhear, I got the impression that there might have been someone . . . someone on the side. They seemed to have some private joke about her liking tea, but I don't know any more than that."

"I see," I said.

Zack took a sandwich. "Are you working with the police on this?" he asked after taking a bite. "Somebody said something to me about you being a police detective."

"Not anymore," I said, as I helped myself to a chicken and dill sandwich. "I retired a few years ago. However, the lead detective on the case is my old partner, and Harper asked me to help out with the investigation in any way I could."

Zack popped the rest of the sandwich into

his mouth and swallowed it in one gulp. "This is so surreal," he said. "I mean, Dan could be difficult at times, but I can't see why anyone would want to kill him."

"He definitely could be difficult," I agreed. "How did you like working for him?"

Zack regarded me warily. "He was a great critic and knew the theater inside and out. He could be opinionated, and we didn't always see eye-to-eye, but I was learning a lot from him."

"What kind of things did you differ on, if you don't mind me asking?"

Zack shrugged. "Oh, nothing big. The quality of some stage productions, the trend of placing Shakespeare's plays in modern day, that sort of thing."

"Is that what you were arguing about at the afterparty?" I asked.

Zack's eyes widened. "What? Who said we were arguing?"

"Are you saying you weren't?" I countered.

Zack took a sip of his tea before answering. "No," he said slowly. "I'm not saying that, but it wasn't a big deal or anything. Just a difference of opinion."

"About what?" I prodded.

"It was nothing, really. Just something to do with his book."

"The one featuring his old reviews?" I asked.

Zack nodded. "Yes. But he was also adding in various stories and anecdotes about certain stars. I was helping him edit it, and I disagreed with a story he wanted to include."

"What was the story?" I asked.

Zack looked as if he were about to refuse to tell me, then he sighed and said, "It was a story about Brooke Casey. I'm not even sure if it's true, and it just seemed to me a bit unfair to include a story that could be nothing more than malicious gossip."

"What was the story?" I asked again.

Zack fiddled with his spoon before answering. "Twelve years ago, Brooke tried out for the lead in *Annie.* She lost the part to a girl named Sally Martin, but she was cast an extra in the orphanage as well as Sally's understudy. During a rehearsal the day before the play opened on Broadway, Sally lost her footing during a dance routine and fell off the stage, breaking her leg in the process. Shattering it, really. Brooke took over the role and her career took off after that. The press loved her, especially once they found out that just like Little Orphan Annie, Brooke was also adopted. Sally, however, didn't fair so well. She had to have six surgeries on her leg and even then, it was never the same. The injury effectively ended her dancing career."

Zack paused and rubbed the edge of his linen napkin between his thumb and forefinger. "At the time, Sally claimed that someone pushed her off the stage and that the someone was Brooke Casey. However, no one who was at the rehearsal saw anything to back up her claims. Sally fell into a bad way after that. She got into drugs and her acting became erratic. No one wanted to work with her anymore. When she turned eighteen, she committed suicide by throwing herself off the top of her apartment building."

"How horrible," I said.

Zack nodded. "I know. Anyway, there have always been people who have whispered behind Brooke's back that maybe she did push Sally off the stage. Dan wanted to include the story in his book. I disagreed. I didn't think it was fair to dredge up old gossip, especially when that gossip was totally without merit."

"What did Dan say?" I asked.

Zack shifted uncomfortably in his chair. "He said that the story wasn't without merit. He said he'd come across someone who was at the rehearsal that day and swears they saw Brooke shove Sally."

"Did he say who?"

Zack shook his head. "He wouldn't tell me. I said whoever it was couldn't be trusted, because if it were true why wouldn't they have come out when it happened? But Dan wouldn't listen. He said he believed the story and was going to include it in the book."

"Did Brooke know that Dan was going to include the story?" I asked. It didn't seem like the Dan I knew to have such power over someone and not abuse it.

Zack shook his head. "No," he said a little too adamantly. "Absolutely not. I was the only one who knew what was in the book. Not all of the stories were favorable, and Dan didn't want anyone to catch wind of what stories he was including. He was afraid certain people might object and takes measures to prevent its publication."

I stared at my teacup for a moment and asked, "Where is the draft of Dan's book now? Do you have it?"

Zack shook his head. "No. I dropped off the latest copy at his apartment a few days ago. I assume it's still there."

I didn't share his optimism.

TWENTY-SEVEN

On the morning of Dan's funeral, I woke up with a mild headache. While Nigel called down to room service for breakfast, I pulled back the heavy brocade drapes. The view that met me was bleak. Heavy gray clouds blanketed the sky. Fat drops of rain splattered down in a haphazard path. I slid open the window as far as it would go and was rewarded with a face full of unseasonably warm, muggy air. I quickly slid the glass back into place. Thinking of the only black dress I'd packed, I scowled. The wool sheath was definitely funeral-appropriate; unfortunately, it was also intended for much cooler temperatures.

Nigel finished placing our order and hung up the phone. "Quick question," I said as I hunted for Skippy's leash. "Would you happen to know Miss Manners' thoughts on wearing panty hose to a funeral?"

Nigel leaned back against the headboard

and regarded me curiously. "That is so weird," he said as he crossed his arms over his chest. "I was just going to ask you the same question."

"Really?" I said as I continued my search.

"Yes," he said. "As you know, the fishnet does wonders for my legs . . ."

"They do indeed," I agreed after a search under the bed proved futile.

"But the black sheer might be a bit more . . ." He paused.

"Appropriate?" I offered as I began to pull up the cushions on the chairs.

Nigel snapped his fingers. "That's it. Appropriate. Why were *you* asking?"

"Oh, for the same reason," I said as I moved my search to the bathroom.

"What are you looking for?" Nigel called out.

"Skippy's leash."

"Try the tub," he suggested.

I did as instructed, and sure enough there it was. I came out of the bathroom and held it up. "You were right," I said.

"I usually am."

"Why the tub, I wonder?" I said as I hooked the leash to Skippy's collar.

"We're slowly working up to a bubbly bath," Nigel said as he got off the bed. "Here, give him to me," he said. "I'll take him. It's disgusting out."

I smiled my thanks. Once they left, I flopped back onto the bed and stared at the ceiling. My mood began to match the weather. I had a grim suspicion that it was only a matter of time before Harper was considered a "person of interest." Now that the higher-ups started to clamor for an arrest, I knew from experience that one was usually made. And that experience also told me that the right person wasn't always arrested.

I was still frowning at the ceiling when Nigel and Skippy returned. They both shook the damp from their respective coats. Skippy then jumped up and joined me on the bed, laying his large wet head across my stomach. Nigel plopped down on my other side and stared at the ceiling with me. "Bloody Mary for your thoughts," he said.

"I thought the saying was *penny* for your thoughts."

"Do you want a penny?" he asked.

"Not particularly," I admitted.

"Thus the Bloody Mary."

"I see your point," I said.

"I thought you might," said Nigel. "So what's wrong? Are you still trying to decipher Miss Manners' stance on panty hose? If you'd rather, I'll wear pants and you can wear the hose."

"You're sweet, but I'm worried about Harper," I said as I played with Skippy's ears. "Marcy is getting pressure to make an arrest. Brian already thinks that Harper's guilty. I just have a bad feeling."

Nigel reached down and grabbed my hand. Linking his fingers with mine, he gave my hand a gentle squeeze. "I know you do," he said. "But all we can do is try to find out what really happened and be there for Harper."

I let out a sigh. "God, I just wish, for Harper's sake, that this day was over. She has to bury her husband, a man who was apparently cheating on her, and who was *murdered,* but she also has to deal with Dan's mother, Cindy. I'm not sure which of the three is worse."

"Is Dan's mother that bad?" Nigel asked.

"She's horrible," I said. "She's a narcissistic, snobby, overbearing social climber."

"She sounds like she'd get along with my Aunt Olive," Nigel said.

I laughed. "Trust me. Cindy would eat Aunt Olive for breakfast."

Nigel let out a low whistle. "Wow. Is it bad that I'm looking forward to meeting this woman?"

"It's your funeral," I said with a shrug.

Nigel leaned over and lightly kissed me. "Actually, it's Dan's, but I get your point."

TWENTY-EIGHT

Dan's funeral was at St. Patrick's Cathedral. Nigel and I were running late due to an unfortunate incident involving Skippy, a novice hotel employee, and an unattended room service cart. It was later agreed to by all parties that bacon would no longer be delivered to our floor.

When we finally arrived, we rushed through the famed bronze doors and straight into Dan's mother, Cindy. A thin, petite woman with ramrod posture and a skull-like face, she always reminded me of an older, meaner version of Mrs. Danvers. Her dark hair was hidden under a black pillbox hat, her perpetual scowl under the matching black-netted veil.

"Hello, Mrs. Trados," I said, putting out my hand. "I'm not sure if you remember me. I'm Nicole Martini. I went to school with Harper. I'm so sorry for your loss."

Cindy stared at me a beat and then extended her hand. "Oh, yes. Aren't you the one who's a security guard or something?" she asked with a sniff.

I forced a smile. "Sort of. I used to be a detective with the New York Police Department," I said. "I'm now retired."

"I'm glad to hear it," she said with a nod. "That's not a proper job for a woman, no matter *what* her particular background."

I nodded. "Yes. I remember you telling me that."

Cindy sniffed again. "Well, I'm glad you finally took my advice." Her gimlet gaze slid to Nigel, and her icy features thawed a tad. "And who is this?" she asked.

"This is my husband," I said. "Nigel Martini."

Nigel smiled and took Cindy's hand in his. "I'm so sorry to have to meet you under these circumstances, Mrs. Trados," he said. "You have my deepest sympathy."

Cindy nodded her thanks. "Martini?" she repeated, her eyes lighting up a little. "Are you perhaps related to Audrey Martini?"

Nigel nodded. "She's my cousin."

Cindy's demeanor thawed even further. Nigel's family is quite well known and quite wealthy — two of Cindy's favorite characteristics. So much so that over the years she began to sprinkle famous celebrities into her conversation, as in "I read where Julie Andrews drinks the same tea that I do." After a time, Cindy made the stories more personal. She now indiscriminately tossed about celebrity names with a breathtaking inattentiveness to reality.

"Well, how kind of you to come, Nigel," she said her mouth stretching into a horrible facsimile of a smile. "And please call me Cindy." She let out a little sigh. "It's all so terrible. I don't quite know what I am going to do." She shook her head. "To find out that someone *killed* my Dan! It's just been a nightmare!" She pressed two perfectly manicured fingers against her bright red mouth a moment before continuing. "Of course, as my dear friend Barbara Streisand told me yesterday, I must keep up my usual positive outlook. But it's so hard! The police, of course, have been most unhelpful." She paused here to glare at me. "I would have thought they would have arrested *someone* by now."

"I'm sure they are doing their best, Mrs. Trados," I said. I debated calling her Cindy, as she had invited Nigel to do, but suspected that his was a unique offer.

"Well, their 'best' is clearly not good enough," she snapped. "And I am not alone in thinking that. When I was lunching with

Liz Taylor the other day, she told me she was just horrified at how the police are handling this case."

Next to me, Nigel began to cough. "I am sorry," I said, forcing myself to keep a straight face. "Would you happen to know where Harper is?"

Cindy gestured a bony arm to an area behind her. "I believe that she's off brooding in the Baptistery," she said. "Really, with her upbringing you'd think she'd know better than to skulk off and leave her guests to fend for themselves."

"I'm sure everyone will understand," I said. "I can't imagine anyone expects Harper to entertain them today."

Cindy crinkled her nose as if I'd just waved a dead fish under it. "Yes, well, perhaps they do things differently where *you* come from," she said with a scowl. "Now, if you'll excuse me, I need to see about the music." She briefly laid her hand on Nigel's arm before she turned away and murmured, "Bless you for coming."

"She seems sweet," Nigel said as we watched her stomp down the aisle.

"So is cyanide, I hear."

"Do you think someone should mention to her that Elizabeth Taylor died?" Nigel asked.

I stared at him in disbelief. "Are you kidding? That's the only thing that makes it bearable for Harper to deal with Cindy. Last time Harper saw her, Cindy told her that she'd just had dinner with Jackie Collins."

"Must have been some dinner," Nigel said.

TWENTY-NINE

Harper was in the Baptistery, as Cindy had said, sitting alone under a canopy of gilded, carved oak. Her face was pale and drawn, and her black Chanel suit sagged in places. Seeing us, she gave us a wan smile and stood up. "Thank God you're here," she said as she pulled me into a tight hug.

"How are you holding up?" I asked.

"By a fraying thread," Harper replied.

"Where's Gracie?" I asked.

"Devin has her," she said as she ran a distracted hand through her hair. "I swear, I'd be a complete mess if it weren't for him. I feel like I'm living in a nightmare, and that was *before* Cindy got here." Harper paused and closed her eyes. "I'd actually forgotten how horrible she is. Within two minutes of her arrival, it all came rushing back in vivid Technicolor." Harper sighed. "Did you know that before my wedding she sent me a detailed diet plan, so I wouldn't look, as she so helpfully put it, 'hippy.' "

I smothered a laugh.

"And don't get me started on her behavior when I was pregnant," she continued. "She sent me article after article about how it was important to remember that pregnancy is a stressful time for the father-to-be, and that I should be a little more mindful of *Dan's* needs."

I stared at her. "You're making that up," I said.

"I most certainly am not," Harper said. "I had it laminated, actually. I thought I could use it at her commitment hearing. I'm going to call it Exhibit A."

"I may have your Exhibit B," I said. "Apparently she had lunch with Elizabeth Taylor."

Harper stared at me in confusion.

"Last week," I clarified.

Harper gave a wan smile. "I take it that you saw her?"

I nodded. "Just now."

Harper craned her neck and peered over my shoulder "Is she still lurking by the doors?" she asked.

"I think so. Why? Did you want me to get her?"

Harper glared at me. "Bite your tongue. She's been hovering by those doors all morning like Cerberus guarding the gates of hell. I couldn't take her anymore so I came here to hide."

"I'm sorry, Harper," I said. "She's not staying with you, is she?"

"No, thank God," said Harper, her eyes widening in mild horror at the thought. "She insisted that I put her up at The Pierre. She needs to be alone in her grief." Harper paused. "Well that, and apparently Burt Reynolds stays there whenever he's in town, and she hasn't seen him in ages," she amended.

"Now that you mention it," said Nigel, "neither have I. Do me a favor, Harper, if she does bump into him, let me know. That son-of-a-bitch owes me money."

Harper laughed and I wrapped my arm around her shoulders. "Listen, Harper," I said, "I'm sorry to bring this up now, but did Dan ever talk to you about the book he was working on?"

"You mean his book of reviews?" she asked.

I nodded. "Yes. He mentioned something at dinner that night about adding anecdotes about various celebrities."

"What about it?" she asked.

"Did he ever tell you about any of the stories?" I asked.

Harper shrugged. "Bits and pieces. He was being pretty secretive about them, to be honest. It was very unlike him, actually. I don't think I need to tell you how much Dan liked to crow about his insider knowledge." Harper frowned at me. "Why do you ask? Do you think his book had something to do with his death?"

"I'm not sure," I admitted. "But I wonder if Dan might have been using the book as a kind of leverage over people."

"Leverage?" she repeated. "What kind of leverage?"

"Well, I just wondered if maybe he could have been using the stories as a bargaining tool to solicit investors for his play," I said gently.

Harper winced and closed her eyes in embarrassment. "That sounds exactly like something he would do. Oh Dan," she whispered. "You dumb, greedy bastard." After a moment, she opened her eyes and looked at me. "I swear, Nic, I had no idea."

I gave her a side hug. "I know you didn't. I just wondered if you remember any of the stories."

"Just one. It was about Nina," she said.

"She had a baby, didn't she?" I guessed.

Harper opened her eyes wide. "Yes, but how did you know?"

I smiled. "Normally I'd tell you that it was because I'm a brilliant detective, but we are in a church so it seems foolish to tempt fate." Harper laughed. "At Peggy's after-party you spoke to Nina as if she'd also had a baby. You played it off as a symptom of baby mush brain, but I saw your face. You weren't confused, you were embarrassed."

Harper nodded. "I felt so stupid. I remember Nina's face after I said that. She looked terrified."

"Do you know when she had the baby?" I asked.

Harper shook her head. "No. I just know that Dan found out that she'd had it and then gave it up for adoption. I don't even know if it was a boy or a girl."

Suddenly the sounds of waves crashing on the shore began to play over the sound system. Harper closed her eyes again as if to shut it out.

"Um . . . what's with the ocean sound-track?" Nigel asked.

Harper's shoulders sagged. "That would be Cindy."

Nigel gave a slow nod as a seagull cawed from above. "Okay," he said slowly. "I'm still not getting this."

"And why would you?" Harper asked with a rueful laugh. "Apparently, Cindy found some quote John F. Kennedy once made before an America's Cup race. Something about how we're all tied to the sea. She decided to use it as inspiration for the theme of the funeral. Can you believe it? A *theme.* Who has a *theme* at a funeral?"

"I'm sorry, Harper. I really am," I said.

Harper let out a frustrated groan. "You have no idea what a nightmare she's been. She's trying to turn Dan's funeral into some kind of social coup."

"Forgive me for asking, but how does one turn a funeral into a social coup?" Nigel asked.

Harper shook her head. "I'm not completely sure. I just know that she's trying to copy President Kennedy's funeral. You saw her hat, right? I think she's cast herself into the role of Jackie." Harper closed her eyes. "It took everything I had to talk her out of a rider-less horse with boots reversed in the stirrups."

I felt my mouth gape open. "You are kidding, right?" I asked.

Harper gave a weary shake of her head. "I wish I were."

The three of us fell silent as a rolling crescendo of crashing waves and the faint cries of seagulls surrounded us. As strange as it was to hear sounds of the tide slamming onto the beach from inside St. Patrick's, it was nothing compared to what happened next. The very distinct sound of a jackhammer began to resonate through out the church.

I looked over to Harper. "What is that?" I asked.

Harper let out a sigh. "That would be the water main that burst on East 51st Street. They've been at it all morning."

We all fell silent as the bone-jarring blasts of the jackhammer began to alternate with the sounds of crashing waves and squawking seagulls. After a moment, Nigel put his arm around Harper's shoulders and lightly kissed her temple. "I think this should be your Exhibit A," he said.

THIRTY

To say that Dan's funeral service was memorable would be like saying the *Titanic* had a rough crossing. Cindy's response to unrelenting bursts from the jackhammer was to increase the volume on her ocean soundtrack. The end result was that for nearly an hour, Dan's mourners listened to what sounded like an audio of seagulls armed with heavy machine guns, engaged in a bloody battle.

Following the service, we headed to Sardi's for the reception. Inside the famed Broadway institution, waiters in red jackets and black pants guided guests to the main dinning room. There, against deep red walls, over 1,200 caricatures of show-business celebrities smiled down at us.

Nigel and I spied Brooke and Mark by the bar and wandered over their way. Their heads were bent close together, but when they saw us approaching they moved apart.

I thought about the story that Zack had told me about Brooke and wondered if it could be true. As I did, Brooke smiled warmly at us and gestured for us to join them. It seemed inconceivable that the charming woman in front of me could have been so cruel as to destroy another girl's career.

Nigel caught the bartender's attention and asked for two glasses of wine. Mark waited until Nigel had finished ordering before offering a tentative smile and shaking Nigel's hand, saying, "It's Nigel, right? I'm Mark Adams. We spoke briefly at Fletcher's the other night."

Nigel nodded. "I remember. Sorry to see you again under these circumstances."

Mark gave a grim smile. "I still can't wrap my head around all of this. I heard that the police definitely think that Dan was murdered?" he asked, his glance sliding to mine. I gave an affirming nod. Mark shook his head as in disbelief.

"This all seems like a dream," Brooke said with a small shudder. "Or rather a nightmare."

"To think that someone actually killed him," Mark said. "I mean, he wasn't the most well-liked guy — he seemed to get a kick out of being critical for the sake of being critical. And he definitely pissed people off with some of his reviews, but I can't see why anyone would want to kill him just because of that."

"I think it's hard for most people to understand the motive behind anyone's killing," I said. "People still do it every day."

"But he was just a theater critic," Mark protested. "So what if he gave a play — or an actress — a crappy review?" Beside him, Brooke began to fidget uncomfortably. "I mean, really," Mark went on. "In the scheme of things, who cares? It's one review. Nobody's career ever tanked because of one lousy review."

"Mark, I really don't think that's fair —" Brooke began.

"Yes, but the police said —" Mark began.

"Actually, I don't think the police have established that he was killed because of one of his reviews," I said.

Brooke glanced at me with a relieved expression. "See, Mark?" she said. "You can't just assume that Dan was murdered because of a review."

Mark blinked. "Right. I know," he said. "It's just . . . well, you can't deny that he made some enemies over the years with his barbs."

I took a sip of my wine. "Are you thinking of anyone in particular?"

Brooke tensed. Mark gave what I'm sure he thought was an indifferent shrug. He'd been wise to focus on directing; an actor he was not. "No," he said. "I mean, I'm not. I've heard other people make some guesses, but it seems unfair."

"That's because most people are gossipy idiots," said a familiar voice behind us. I turned to see Nina standing with a drink in one hand and a challenging look in her eyes.

Mark's face flushed red. "Oh, hello, Nina," he said. "I didn't see you there."

Nina smirked. "Yes. Thanks for the up-date, but I was able to work that out all by myself."

THIRTY-ONE

"Hello, Nina," Brooke said. "Are you feeling better?"

Nina's glance fell on the younger woman. A flash of some emotion I couldn't quite identify crossed her face and then was gone. "I am, actually," she said. "Thank you for asking."

"Do you know what was wrong? I certainly hope it's not contagious," Brooke continued.

"I shouldn't worry, dear. The doctor thought it was food poisoning," Nina said.

Brooke's eyes opened wide. "Food poisoning? How terrible!"

Nina grimaced. "Yes, it was most unpleasant. But I survived."

Brooke leaned forward and placed her hand on Nina's arm. "Well, I'm glad you're back. The play just wasn't right without you."

Next to her Mark nodded. "I have to say I

agree with Brooke," he said to the surprise of no one. "Your understudy, Molly, is a good actress, but her scenes with Brooke just didn't seem to click the way yours do. It's funny how you just get a certain connection with some people, isn't it?"

Nina stared at Mark a beat and then said, "Not really. It's called acting."

Mark gave an awkward cough and then said, "Well, I'm glad you're feeling better."

A young woman in a waitstaff uniform suddenly appeared next to Nina. In her hands was a small silver tea tray. She politely cleared her throat and said, "Your tea, Ms. Durand."

Nina glanced over at the woman and smiled. "Thank you, dear. Please just set it on the bar."

The young woman nodded and set the tray down as indicated. "Shall I pour for you, Ms. Durand?"

Nina shook her head. "No, thank you. I prefer to do it myself."

"Still a control freak about your damn tea, I see," Fletcher's voice suddenly boomed out from behind me.

Nina turned and leveled Fletcher with an icy stare. "Still an egotistical jackass, I see," she countered.

Fletcher's eyes narrowed. "It takes one to

know one, darling."

Nina let out a laugh. "What are you, ten years old?" she scoffed. "But I suppose on a certain level, it makes sense. Your sense of humor is just as underdeveloped as" — here she paused letting her gaze drop before adding — "*other* parts of you."

Brooke began to cough into a napkin. "Sorry," she wheezed when Fletcher glared at her. "I have horrible allergies."

"Really," intoned Fletcher slowly. "What a coincidence. So do I." He glanced from Brooke to Nina and back to Brooke. "However, mine act up in the spring rather than early September. Odd, don't you think?"

Some of the color left Brooke's face, and her eyes darted to Nina. Nina crossed her arms and regarded Fletcher with a bored look. "So let me see if I'm following you correctly," she said. "Since *you* get allergies in the spring, the entire allergy-suffering world must also get them at the same time. Tell me, Fletch, is your physician aware that you suffer from narcissistic delusions?"

Fletcher stared at Nina a beat and then turned and walked off without another word.

"I hope it was something I said," Nina called out after him in a saccharinely sweet voice.

Fletcher's response was brief, nonverbal, and crystal clear. Nina smiled.

Brooke did not.

THIRTY-TWO

Sometime later, Nigel and I wandered over to where Jeremy stood quietly talking with his agent, Julie. They looked like an ad for an edgy, European designer. Jeremy wore an expertly tailored suit of worsted wool. His hair was slicked back with gel to the point that it almost looked polished. Julie was wearing an elegant black sheath that managed to be somber and sexy all at the same time. She wore her hair in a loose upsweep that Nigel referred to as the "naughty secretary." Julie saw us first and discreetly nudged Jeremy to alert him of our presence. Jeremy glanced our way and offered us a small wave.

"So this is pretty horrible," he said by way of a greeting. "I don't think I've ever been to the funeral of someone who was murdered before."

Julie sucked in a sharp breath. "Jeremy!"

she admonished. "What a horrid thing to say!"

Jeremy looked down at her with a blank stare. "What?" he asked. "All I said was that Dan was murdered. It's not like it's a secret or anything. I mean, it's why we're all here."

Julie shot him a quelling look before turning to Nigel and me with an apologetic smile. "You'll have to excuse Jeremy," she said. "He spends so much of his time acting that he sometimes forgets to be human."

Jeremy rolled his eyes and took a sip of his wine. "Oh, so we're just supposed to ignore the elephant in the room?" he asked.

Julie rolled her eyes in exasperation, "Yes, darling. It's called conversing in polite society. You should try it sometime."

"Sounds deadly dull," Jeremy observed before taking another sip from his glass.

Julie shot him a censorious look before turning to me. "How is Harper doing?" she asked. "I was only able to speak to her briefly at the funeral. And of course a receiving line is no place for a heart-to-heart."

I took a sip of my own drink before answering. "She's doing well, all things considered," I said. "To be honest, I think it's Gracie that's kept her sane. She won't allow herself to fall apart because she knows Gracie needs her."

Julie nodded. "She is an adorable baby." There was a pause as all of us took a sip of our respective drinks. "By the way, who is the young man helping Harper with Gracie?" Julie asked, her voice casual.

"That's Devin," I answered, in an equally causally tone. "Gracie's nanny."

Next to me Jeremy sputtered. "That's one hell of an ugly nanny."

"Well, he's a guy, so I think that might have something to do with it," Nigel offered.

Julie glared at Jeremy. "For God's sake, Jeremy," she hissed. "Think before you speak."

Jeremy blinked at Julie. "I was kidding, Jules," he said. "Chill."

Julie sighed and shook her head. "Why do I even bring you out in public?" she asked herself. "You're nothing but a walking social gaffe."

Jeremy produced a crooked smile and blew her a kiss. "Yes, but I'm a walking social gaffe that looks good in a suit," he countered.

Nigel nodded in understanding. "That's the only reason I get out as often as I do," he said.

Julie laughed and then turned back to me. "So the nanny, huh?" she said before shifting her focus to where Devin now stood with a sleeping Gracie snuggled up against his chest. "Damn. He almost makes child-birth seem worth it," she said.

Jeremy snorted. "Not going to happen," he said.

Julie's eye's narrowed in annoyance. "I don't see how you have any say in that, *Jeremy,*" she said, her voice now an icy blast.

Jeremy glanced down and mumbled an embarrassed apology. Julie shook her head and muttered something that sounded like "jackass." Perhaps in an attempt to change the conversation, Jeremy turned to me, say-ing, "So you used to work with the detec-tive that's investigating Dan's case."

I nodded. "Marcy and I were partners for about five years," I said. "We worked Homi-cide."

"Why did you leave the Department?" Jeremy asked.

"The abridged version is that I got shot and ended up on desk duty," I said. "The desk and I didn't suit."

Jeremy's eyebrows lifted in interest. "What the unabridged version?" he asked.

"I got shot in the leg and ended up on desk duty," I said.

Jeremy let out a short bark of laughter. "Touché," he said. "Well, seeing as how you know the lead detective, have you heard if the police have any idea who killed Dan?"

Julie's head snapped up at Jeremy's question. "They have a few leads," I said with a noncommittal shrug. "But nothing concrete yet. Actually, you two probably would know more than I do. I mean, the theater community is pretty tight. What have you heard?"

Julie and Jeremy exchanged a cautious glance. "Oh, not much really," Jeremy said.

I raised an eyebrow. "Oh, come on," I scoffed. "I know from Peggy that life amongst the theater crowd is a gossip's dream come true."

Jeremy shrugged. "That may be so, but I don't feel comfortable slamming a guy at his own funeral. I mean, none of us are perfect. Hell, I'm living proof of that."

Julie clinked her wineglass against his. "Cheers to that," she said wryly.

"Oh, I know," I said. "But don't forget, I knew Dan, too. He wasn't an easy guy to get along with. You're not going to offend me by repeating something negative." Jeremy eyed me doubtfully. "For instance, what are people saying about his affairs?" I asked.

Jeremy stared at me blankly. "Affairs?" he repeated.

"You know, with other women," I said. Jeremy continued to stare at me in silence. "With woman who were not his wife," I amended.

Jeremy shook his head. "I don't know what you're talking about," he said. "Dan was known to be something of an ass, but I never heard anything about him cheating on Harper." He glanced questioningly at Julie.

She too shook her head. "First I've ever heard of it," she said.

"Really?" I said. "That's interesting."

THIRTY-THREE

I was glad when Harper arrived with her father. Donald Remington was a tall, distinguished man with a broad face, a ready smile, and a thick mane of silver hair. He was fiercely devoted to his family and had been devastated when Harper's mother died last year. Since Diana's death, Harper said that Donald focused much of his attention and time on her and Gracie. The result was that Donald came to loathe his son-in-law. Now that other unsavory aspects of Dan's extracurricular activities had apparently come to light, it was a good thing that somebody had killed Dan. Otherwise, Donald would have done it himself.

Nigel and I made our way over to their side. Donald smiled when he saw me and pulled me into one of his trademark bear hugs. "Nicole!" he said. "It's so good to see you. How have you been?"

I smiled back. "We've been just fine," I

said. "Donald, you remember my husband, Nigel?"

"Of course I do," Donald said as the two men shook hands.

"It's good to see you again, sir," Nigel said. "Sorry it has to be under these circumstances."

Donald nodded his head sharply and glanced at Harper. "I swear to God, it took every ounce of my self-control not to stand up during the service and announce to everyone just what kind of man Dan really was," he said.

Harper closed her eyes. "Dad," she began.

Donald raised his large hand as if to stop her protests. "I know, pumpkin, I know. It wouldn't have been appropriate, which is why I didn't say anything. But damn if that mother of his didn't try my last nerve with her eulogy. Seriously, I don't think I've ever heard so many lies told from the altar of a church before."

"How are you holding up, Harper?" I asked.

Harper shrugged. "As well as can be expected. I feel numb, to tell you the truth."

I smiled. "That's probably for the best, actually. You can have a lovely breakdown later when you don't have an audience."

Harper gave a hollow laugh. "Is it weird

that that sounds wonderful?"

"Not at all," I said.

"Harper!" a voice boomed out from behind us. Turning, I saw Fletcher striding our way. With him was a striking young woman I guessed to be in her mid-twenties. She had long auburn hair and green eyes that tilted up at the corners. "Harper, I am so sorry for your loss," Fletcher said as he took her hands in his. "I was just dumbfounded when I heard the news. Is there anything you need, my dear?"

Harper shook her head. "No, but thank you. I'm fine. Or at least, I will be."

Fletcher looked searchingly at her face a moment before releasing her hands. The young woman stepped forward and extended her hand. "I'm Pamela," she said, in a childish voice. "I'm, like, really sorry someone killed your husband. That must, like, suck."

Harper's eyes widened. Pamela smiled and quickly shook Harper's hand before stepping back next to Fletcher. Fletcher patted the young woman on her shoulder and said, "Why don't you get us something to drink, Pamela? I'll be with you in a minute."

Pamela nodded and gave us all a carefree wave as she wandered toward the bar. Once she was out of earshot, Harper turned back to Fletcher. "Pamela, huh? What happened to Ruby?" she asked.

Fletcher's brows pulled together. "Who?" he asked.

"Ruby," Harper repeated. "She was at your house the other night."

Fletcher continued to frown as he tried to make the connection. Finally, Nigel said, "You might remember her as Rosie," Nigel said.

Fletcher's face cleared in recognition. "Oh, yes. Rosie! I'm not sure where she is," he said. "Haven't really seen her since that night."

Harper smiled knowingly. "I see. Well, Fletcher, I'd like you to meet my father, Donald," she said as she turned to introduce the two men.

Fletcher looked at Donald in surprise. After a quick appraising glance, he held his hand out. "Pleasure to see you," he said. "Sorry it's under these circumstances. You probably don't remember me, but we met once before a very long time ago. I knew your late wife, Diana. I was so sorry to hear of her passing. She was a lovely woman."

Donald nodded as he shook Fletcher's hand. "I do remember you, of course. Thank you. Diana was very special."

Both men nodded once more as if to

confirm the truth of this statement and released their grips. Fletcher turned his attention back to Harper. "Now, my dear," he said. "Forgive me if I'm being crass, but have the police made any progress in the case yet?"

Harper shook her head. "Not that I'm aware of. They have only confirmed that Dan was poisoned."

Fletcher stared intently at Harper. "Poison?" he repeated. "How . . . odd."

Harper raised a questioning eyebrow. "Odd? Why is it odd?"

Fletcher blinked. "I don't know," he said slowly. "Forgive me. I suppose the whole situation is just hard for me to get my head around. A death when one is so young always rattles." He took her hand in his. "Well, I won't keep you, my dear. But please know how terribly sorry I am about all of this, and if there is anything I can do, please don't hesitate to call." Releasing her hand, he turned to Donald. "Don," he said. "It was good to see you again. You've got an amazing daughter. She's so much like her mother. I hope to see you both again under more pleasant circumstances."

"Thank you," Donald said.

Fletcher nodded to Nigel and me before leaving to search for Pamela. When he was gone, Donald turned to Harper and rolled his eyes. "God, but he was always an ass. Your mother couldn't stand him," he said. "Who the hell brings a date to a funeral, anyway?"

THIRTY-FOUR

Nigel and I had just returned to our hotel room, when my cell phone rang. It was Marcy. "What's up?" I said.

"Hi, Nic," she said, her voice tight.

An uneasy sensation slid down my spine. "I know that tone," I said. "That's your bad news tone. What's happened?"

Marcy let out a sigh and then lowered her voice. "You're not going to like it, but we got a copy of the security footage from Dan's apartment building."

I sat down in the desk chair. Skippy came over and put his head in my lap. I began to robotically stroke his fur. "Okay. What did you find?"

"Your friend Harper was lying when she said that she'd never been to his apartment," Marcy said. "She went there the Friday before he was killed."

I closed my eyes in frustration. I had told Harper to tell the police everything. Apparently she hadn't listened. I let out a sigh. "Damn it," I said. "What else was on the tape? Did anyone else visit Dan?"

"Actually, yes. Seems he was quite popular," Marcy said. "Well, until someone killed him, that is."

"Yes, I guess that could be seen as a turning point. So who else paid him a visit?"

I heard a paper rustle as Marcy looked for the names. "Let's see," she said. "Zack Weems was a frequent visitor. But we knew about him already. He was working with Dan on the manuscript."

"Right. Did you find it?"

"That's another reason I wanted to call you. I didn't find a manuscript," she said.

I frowned. "What do you mean, you didn't find it?"

"I mean, there wasn't any manuscript in the apartment. I even went back and double-checked myself. There's nothing. And when I say, 'nothing,' I actually mean 'nothing.' "

"I'm not following you," I admitted.

"It's just that for a so-called 'work apartment,' there was a strange paucity of work. As in, there was nothing work-related there at all. No files, no plays, no reviews, no correspondence, and definitely no manuscript.

"Have you interviewed Zack yet? What did he say about it?" I asked.

"He says he dropped off the latest copy of the manuscript on Thursday night, which checks with the security footage. He seemed pretty surprised that it wasn't there. He wondered if perhaps Dan had brought it home," she said.

"I'll ask Harper," I said.

"I already did," Marcy said with a half laugh. "She said there is no copy at the house. I gather that Dan planned on including certain stories about various celebrities in his book. According to Zack, some of them bordered on libelous. He had been trying to convince Dan not to include them in the final copy. I think he was afraid of the blowback and being tarnished with guilt by association."

"Zack told me that as well," I said. "Dan had heard some gossip about Brooke Casey that Zack didn't want included. I got the impression it wasn't so much that he thought it was morally wrong, as that he has a crush on Brooke."

Marcy laughed. "Yeah. I got that impression, too. So after Zack, we have Jeremy Hamlin. He visited Dan on Wednesday."

"Did he say why?" I asked.

"Mr. Hamlin indicated that it was a business meeting to discuss a play that Dan was producing," said Marcy. She paused.

"What aren't you telling me?" I asked.

"I don't know," she said. "He was very forthcoming when we interviewed him, but when we first told him about the security tape, I got the impression he had no idea what we were talking about."

"As in he didn't know what a security tape was?" I asked.

"No, more like he didn't remember going to Dan's in the first place," said Marcy. "He claimed that the shock of Dan's murder had rattled him and it was all very believable, but . . ." Marcy trailed off.

"But what?" I prompted.

"But the guy is an actor, after all," she explained. "It just made me wonder."

"Okay," I said. "Anyone else?"

"Yes, Nina Durand visited Dan twice that week. Once on Tuesday and once on Thursday."

I sat up a bit straighter. "Well, that's interesting. I wonder if Nina is our tea drinker?"

"She is," Marcy said. "She was completely upfront about their relationship when we interviewed her. Said that it was a brief fling but that it had ended amicably."

"And you believed her?" I asked.

Marcy paused. "I think so?"

"Are you asking *me*?"

Marcy let out a sigh. "I believe her and I don't. I honestly didn't get the sense that she was pining over the man. But I do think there's something she's not telling us."

"Anything else?"

"There is, but I'm not sure if it's connected to the murder," said Marcy. "Around three a.m. on the day of the murder, a cloaked figure entered the building. Couldn't tell if it was male or female. But whoever it was wasn't buzzed in. They punched in the building code, so it could have been one of the other tenants. About a half hour later, the same figure exited the building. We've interviewed all the tenants, and so far no one has come forward to say it was them."

"Curious," I said.

"I thought so," said Marcy. "Of course, one of the tenants could have had a visitor that they didn't want anyone to know about. It could be completely unrelated to the murder."

"It could be, but that's a hell of a coincidence, don't you think?"

"I do," agreed Marcy.

I was silent for a moment. "So in addition to Harper, Zack, Nina, and Jeremy visited

Dan's apartment."

"Right, but only Harper lied about it. That's the problem," Marcy said. "Brian is convinced that she's guilty."

"And what about you?"

She sighed. "I don't agree with him. I think we're still missing something."

"Well, that's a good thing, right?"

"Not really," she said. "Brian made his case to the Captain and he agrees."

"Put it in English for me, Marcy."

She sighed. "The judge just granted a warrant for Harper's arrest."

"What?" I yelled. "Seriously? When?" I abruptly stood up, knocking Skippy's head off my lap in the process. He shot me a baleful stare.

"A half hour ago," Marcy said apologetically. "It's happening now."

"Shit," I said, closing my eyes.

"Listen, Nic, I'm not saying that I think she's innocent, but I will admit that my gut is telling me I'm missing something."

I rubbed my hand over my face. "Damn it. She didn't do it," I said, more to myself than her. "Okay. Anything else?"

"Well, I'm not sure if this is anything important," she said, "but we did find an interesting contact on Dan's phone."

"Yeah? Who?"

"Frank Little," she said.

"Seriously?" I said. "Dan was in touch with our favorite sociopathic loan shark?"

"It would seem so," Marcy said.

"Are he and Danny still running Little's Vittles?" I asked.

"As far as I know the Board of Health hasn't shut it down," said Marcy. "I shudder to think how bad a restaurant has to be before they take action."

"I think I might be in the mood for some bad Italian food," I said after a minute.

"I figured as much," Marcy said in a resigned voice. "Just promise me you'll be careful."

"About the food or the servers?" I asked.

"Both."

"Don't worry, I promise to be careful," I said.

Marcy let out a dubious sigh. "I know. I just worry that one day it'll be a promise you can't keep."

THIRTY-FIVE

After hanging up with Marcy, I called Harper's house. There was no answer. I then called her cell phone. On the fifth ring, Devin picked up. He sounded horrible. "Devin?" I said. "It's Nic Martini. I was trying to reach Harper."

"She's not here, Ms. Martini," he said his voice a breathless rush. "The police came. They . . . they arrested her. They arrested Harper." His voice caught. "They think she had something to do with Dan's . . . Mr. Trados's death. I told them they were wrong. I told them it was impossible. I was here that night. I was here with Harper all night. She never left. But they didn't listen. Jesus. This is a nightmare. I don't know what to do."

"Don't worry, Devin," I said. "We'll take care of it. Now, first things first. Where's Gracie?"

"I have her. I'm going to stay here with her."

"Okay, Devin. That's good. Second question, did someone call Harper's lawyer?"

"Yes," he said. "Her dad is taking care of it. They're going to meet her at the police station."

"Good."

"But how do I help Harper?" he asked his voice desperate. "I mean, she didn't kill Dan. God knows he was horrible to her, but she's too good of a person to ever kill someone. I mean . . ."

"Devin," I interrupted him, "I have to ask you something, and I want you to be honest —"

"Yes," Devin said in a rush, "I love her. I know it probably sounds crazy. There is an age difference . . . but she's an amazing woman. She's like no one I've ever met. But nothing happened. I mean, nothing until . . ."

"Devin," I interrupted him again, a bit firmer this time, "I'm going to ask you to stop talking right now for several reasons, not the least of which is that I want to be able to truthfully say I don't know what happened between you and Harper. The only thing I want to know is whether you were telling me the truth about spending the night at Harper's."

Devin answered immediately. "I was here all night," he said. "I swear."

"Good," I answered. "Did either of you go out without the other that night?"

This time Devin didn't answer immediately. Finally, he said, "I . . . I went to the drug store at one point to get some baby Tylenol."

"How long were you gone?"

"I . . . I'm not sure. The first place I went to didn't have the right kind, so it took me longer than I thought it would."

"How long?" I repeated.

"About forty minutes," he said, his voice barely a whisper.

I thanked Devin and hung up. Forty minutes. Dan's work apartment was only ten minutes from where he and Harper lived. I knew Harper would never leave Gracie alone, but the police might have other ideas.

THIRTY-SIX

I sat back down in the chair and stared unseeingly at the floral arrangement on the table in front of me. "What did Marcy say?" Nigel asked.

"Lots, actually," I said, "but the main thing is that they're arresting Harper."

Nigel's eyes widened in shock. "Are you serious? Then we need to go down there and bail her out," he said.

I held up my hand. "Harper's dad is already on it. He and the family lawyer are on their way to the station now."

Nigel relaxed slightly. "Well, that's good."

I shrugged. "That's a relative term."

Nigel squeezed my shoulder. "Hang on. I know what you need."

Skippy put his head back in my lap and nudged my hand with his nose. I began to pet his ears when he started to whine. Leaning down, I lifted up one ear and peered in. "Nigel," I called. "Did we bring Skippy's medicine? I think he's got another ear infection."

"I'll get it," Nigel said. "Hang on."

Moments later, Nigel appeared with a dirty martini. I glanced up at him. "I hope that's for me, and not Skippy," I said.

"Of course," Nigel said as he set the glass down on the table in front of me. "Skippy likes his martinis dry." Reaching into his pocket, he pulled out a bottle of the ointment. Skippy stoically held still while Nigel put a few drops in each ear. "Good boy, Skippy," he said. "Now don't scratch at them or we'll have to pull out the cone of shame."

Skippy put his head back in my lap and stared mournfully at me. "Okay," I said, "you can have an olive." I fished one out and tossed it to him. Skippy caught it neatly and lay down at my feet.

Nigel went to get his drink and then slid into the chair opposite me. He clinked his glass against mine. I took a grateful sip. "What else did Marcy have to say?" he asked. When I finished telling him, he let out a low whistle. "Damn. This just keeps getting better and better," he said. He took a sip of his drink. "So who do you want to visit first?" he asked.

I looked at him in confusion. "Visit?"

Nigel nodded. "Yes. The way I see it, we need to talk to Nina and Jeremy first thing tomorrow about their visits to Dan. Then maybe we can grab a late lunch."

I smiled at him. "Have I told you today how much I love you?" I asked.

"I believe you covered that subject quite satisfactorily earlier this morning," Nigel said. "But if you feel the need to go over it again, I'm happy to oblige. However in the interest of full disclosure, I probably should tell you *where* I'm taking you to lunch before you embark on any demonstrations of affection."

I sat back in my chair with a slow smile. "I assumed you were taking me to Little's Vittles."

Nigel smiled back. "You are a clever girl."

I tipped my head in acknowledgement. "By the way, thank you for my martini."

"You're welcome. Is it dirty enough for you?"

I took a sip and winked. "Never."

THIRTY-SEVEN

The next morning I came out of the shower to find Skippy sitting in the middle of the hallway. I looked down at him and then yelled, "Nigel! For God's sake, no."

A second later, Nigel came around the corner. "What's wrong?" he asked.

"That's what's wrong," I said pointing at Skippy. During the night, he'd been unable to stop scratching at his ears. This morning we were forced to pull out the cone of shame. However, Nigel had made some modifications to it while I was in the shower. Three olive decals now adorned one side of the plastic cone. "Seriously, Nigel? He looks like a walking martini glass."

Nigel frowned. "And that's bad, why?"

I opened my mouth but realized I didn't have an answer — at least not one that would satisfy Nigel. I closed my mouth and sighed. Nigel grinned at me. "See?" he said. "Besides, Skippy likes it. Don't you, boy?"

Skippy gave a happy bark.

Nigel arched his eyebrow. "Never doubt the power of a Martini," he said as he leaned over and kissed me on the shoulder.

"Are we taking about the drink or you?" I asked, as I readjusted my towel.

"Both," Nigel said as he adjusted it back. "But there is a hierarchy between the two that apparently you need to be reminded of."

"Is that a fact?"

"It is."

Sometime later, after Nigel had expertly made his point, we left to pay Nina a visit. Nigel had called ahead to ask if he could stop by to catch up and reminisce about old times. At my suggestion, he did not mention that Skippy and I would be in attendance.

After Nigel hung up with Nina, I called Marcy. I asked her to give me the dates and times of Nina's visits to Dan's apartment. "Sure," she said. "Mind if I ask why you need them?"

"I have a theory about those visits," I said.

"Is this a theory you plan on sharing?" she asked.

"Only if I'm right," I said.

"Typical," Marcy said with a laugh. "Hang on, let me get the report." A minute later,

Marcy came back on the phone with the dates and times. "Is that what you were looking for?" she asked.

"I sincerely hope so," I said.

Nina lived in a luxury apartment on Central Park South. Outside it was the perfect fall day; the sky was bright blue and the air was clean and crisp. Well, clean and crisp by New York City's standards. Given the weather, we decided to walk the relatively short distance to Nina's. That and the fact that getting a taxi with Skippy was difficult on the best of days. Now that he looked like an alcoholic's hallucination, it was near impossible.

A uniformed doorman outside the apartment building greeted us with a polite nod. It was some credit to his professionalism that he did not gawk at Skippy. Either that or the residents had already jaded him to sights of the absurd.

Inside, a poised young woman of about twenty-five sat at a sleek mahogany desk. She wore the standard corporate uniform of a dark tailored suit with a crisp white blouse. Her thick chestnut hair was pulled back into a severe bun. The only concession to color was a slash of red lipstick. A slim white nametag announced her name as

Marta. She glanced up at our entrance with a polished smile. "Good afternoon," she said in a smooth, practiced voice. "May I help you?"

"Yes," Nigel said with a smile. "Nigel and Nicole Martini to see Ms. Nina Durand."

Marta's eyes briefly slid to Skippy; the only tell of her relative inexperience. Nigel saw the look and quickly added, "And Master Skippy Martini."

She blinked. "But of course. One moment while I ring Ms. Durand." After a brief telephone conversation confirmed our visit was anticipated, Marta smiled at us and nodded toward the elevator. "Ms. Durand is expecting you. She's on the sixtieth floor. The elevators are to your right."

Nigel and I smiled our thanks. Once inside the elevator, I turned to him and said, "I hate to sound like the jealous spouse, but I don't recall anyone telling us what apartment Nina is in."

Nigel laughed and leaned over to kiss me soundly on the lips. "Have I told you today how much I love you?" he asked.

"Yes," I said. "Now answer the damn question."

Nigel raised one eyebrow. "I don't believe you asked one."

I raised one eyebrow right back. "Do you

really want those to be your last words here on earth?"

Nigel leaned down and nipped me on the earlobe. "Nina's apartment is the entire floor," he explained. "The elevator will only open to her apartment."

I raised an eyebrow.

Nigel realized his error and quickly added, "I *assume.*"

I gave a rueful shake of my head. "It's a good thing you're so charming," I said.

Nigel grinned. "But darling, it's because I *am* so charming, that I have to be charming *now.*"

I laughed. "Touché, Nigel. Touché."

THIRTY-EIGHT

Nina did a fairly passable job of pretending that she wasn't expecting a private reunion with Nigel. Of course, she was wearing a black silk robe, and from the looks of it, nothing else, so I was pretty sure my presence was a surprise. At least, I sincerely hoped it was.

"Darling!" she cooed to me after greeting Nigel a shade more enthusiastically than necessary. "I'm so delighted to see you again. And who is this?" she asked, looking down at Skippy.

"This is our dog Skippy," I explained.

"Are you sure he's a dog?" she asked. "He's so big."

"I know," said Nigel. "We suspect that he's wearing lifts, but we haven't been able to catch him."

Nina looked at him and laughed. "Have you been drinking?" she asked.

Nigel shook his head. "No, why? Do you

think I should be?"

Nina laughed again and said, "I'll take that as a hint. Please, make yourselves comfortable." She waved us to take a seat in the living room while she went to the sideboard and poured a generous splash of scotch into a glass. She took a sip and then turned back to us. "So what's your pleasure?" she asked. "I have wine, gin, vodka and, of course, Chivas Regal," she said indicating the bottle in her hand. "If I remember correctly, Nigel, that's one of your favorites."

"It is. Thank you," said Nigel with a nod. "I'm surprised you remembered."

Nina winked. "I have a very good memory," she said.

When she turned back to the sideboard to pour two more glasses, I took the opportunity to flick Nigel on his ear. He smothered a smile and shrugged. Nina turned back, drinks in hand, and walked over to us. "Is it true that the police arrested Harper for Dan's murder?" she asked as she handed us our drinks.

"I'm afraid so," Nigel answered.

Nina suddenly froze. "Oh dear God," she gasped. "Is that why you're here? Did Harper kill Dan because of his affair with *me*?"

"No, it's nothing like that," I said. "Besides, Harper didn't kill Dan."

Nina glanced sharply at me. "Well, you certainly don't think *I* had anything to do with it, do you?"

I smiled. "Of course not," I said. "We're only here because we wanted to ask you a few questions about Dan."

"Well, that, and because you serve an excellent scotch," Nigel said with a wink as he took a sip of his drink.

Nina let out a throaty laugh and curled up on the opposite couch. "Oh Nigel," she said. "You could always make me laugh." She tucked her feet under her legs and arranged the folds of her robe over her legs. "Well, what did you want to know?" she asked.

"How long were you and Dan together?" Nigel asked.

Nina tilted her head. There was no trace of embarrassment as she considered the question. She reacted no differently than if Nigel asked her what she had for dinner last night. "Hmmm," she said as she tapped the edge of her glass with her finger. "Not that long really; a few weeks, maybe. It certainly wasn't *serious*." Suddenly her gaze turned to me. She regarded me for a moment and then said, "I know Harper is your friend, and as such, you probably think I'm horrible."

I shook my head. "Of course not," I said. "And neither does Harper. To be honest, I think she was a bit relieved."

Nina's brows drew together. "She was relieved?" she repeated, her tone puzzled.

Leaning forward a bit in my chair. "Harper told me about Dan's penchant for full-body waxing," I confided. "Between you and me, she *hated* it."

Nina blinked. "Oh," she said. "I see."

I nodded. "So you needn't worry about Harper holding a grudge or anything," I said. "Besides, Dan never made a secret of his affairs."

Nina took a sip of her drink. "Good. I'd hate to think that I was the cause of any additional pain for her."

I shook my head and leaned back in my chair. "Not at all. But I was curious about one thing. Why did Dan give you such a nasty review? Usually his trysts ended amicably."

Nina lifted a slim shoulder before answering. "I may have said a few things that got back to him," she said.

"Things like what?" I asked.

Nina took a sip of her drink before answering. "To be honest, I wasn't a big fan of the

227

waxing either," she said. "I felt like I was making love to a Ken doll."

Next to me Nigel almost spit out his drink.

"I can well imagine," I said.

"Well, luckily, it was a short-lived affair," Nina went on. "I find those are the best."

"Is that why you broke off your engagement with Fletcher Levin?" I asked.

Nina looked startled. "Yes," she finally said. "I was just eighteen and starting my career. I realized that I wasn't cut out for marriage and a family."

"You went to Europe after that, didn't you?"

Nina's lip's tightened and her eyes shuttered. "That's right," she said.

"You were there for about a year, is that right?" I asked.

Nina gave a tight smile. "That's right."

"Were you in a production?" I asked.

Nina took another sip of her drink. "No. I took a little sabbatical," she said with a casual shrug. "Being engaged to Fletcher Levin — even for only a brief time — rather took its toll on me."

I smiled sympathetically. "I quite understand. He strikes me as being somewhat dogmatic in his views about women, especially once they become mothers."

Nina drained the rest of her drink. "You've no idea," she said.

THIRTY-NINE

"Darling," Nigel said once we'd left Nina's building, "the next time you decide to spring a bald-faced lie, no pun intended, about full-body waxing, do you think you could warn me? I almost spit out my drink. And I don't think I need to remind you, that was some damn good scotch."

I laughed. "Sorry about that."

Nigel glanced at me sideways. "It was a lie, though, right?" he asked. "I mean, Dan was bad enough already. But the idea of him . . . *hairless,*" he added with a shudder. "I just can't."

"Yes, it was a lie," I said. "I think Nina said she had an affair with Dan to cover up for the real reason she went to his apartment."

"You think Dan had a story on her like he had on Brooke?" he asked.

"I do," I said. "I just need to figure out what it was."

■ ■ ■ ■

From Nina's, we headed over to Jeremy's. Jeremy lived in a quaint brownstone on Central Park West. It was tucked away on a quiet, tree-lined street. Unlike our visit to Nina, this one was unannounced. Nigel and I suspected that we would have better luck if we caught Jeremy unprepared. We couldn't have asked for better timing. When Jeremy finally answered the door, it was clear from his rumpled appearance that we'd woken him. It was also clear from his bloodshot eyes and the sour smell of alcohol emanating from him that he'd passed out drunk wearing his clothes from the night before. His navy sports coat was beyond wrinkled. His white dress shirt was missing a few buttons. His jeans were undone at the waist. His heavy-lidded eyes rose in surprise at the sight of us on his doorstep. Of course, that may have had more to do with Skippy than us. "Did I know you were coming?" Jeremy asked, his voice gravely.

Before Nigel could answer honestly, I lied and said, "Yes. You don't remember?"

Jeremy blinked and scratched his head. I watched as he tried to summon a memory that wasn't there. When it didn't surface,

Jeremy opted to pretend. "Um . . . no," he said. "I mean yes. Sure. Sorry. I guess I overslept."

I flashed a smile that I hoped resembled sympathetic understanding. "Is now still a good time?" I asked.

Jeremy scratched his stomach. A puzzled expression crossed his face and he looked down at his hand. He seemed surprised to find that he was still wearing his jacket. He looked back up at us. "Um . . . yeah," he said. "Sure. Come on in."

Jeremy led us down a hallway that was covered in photos from his career. All together, they formed a visual timeline of his life on the stage. It was rather depressing, really. Jeremy had once been a good-looking man. But as the pictures testified to, his excessive drinking had steadily eroded those looks. As Jeremy waved at us to take a seat in his living room, I wondered why he was still numbing himself with alcohol. He'd openly stated that his abuse was due to the stress of having to lead a closeted life. Yet he'd recently come out to almost universal support. Why was he still hitting the bottle?

Jeremy sank into a leather club chair while Nigel and I took a seat on the couch. Skippy sat in front of Jeremy and laid his enormous head in his lap. Jeremy stared down at it with a puzzled expression.

"I think he likes you," Nigel said.

"So he's real then?" Jeremy asked as he tentatively reached out and gently patted Skippy's head. Skippy's tail gave a happy thump.

Nigel laughed. "Yes, he's real."

Jeremy nodded. "Thank God. For a minute I really thought I was losing it."

"Well, Skippy has that effect on people sometimes," I said. Granted, it was usually with people whose blood alcohol content was in the double digits, but I thought it might be best if I kept that to myself.

Jeremy nodded again, his attention still on Skippy's head. After a moment, he looked up at us. For a brief second, it looked as if he was surprised to find us sitting in his living room. He gave a slow blink and let out a breath. "So how can I help you?" he asked.

"I wanted to ask you a few questions about Dan," I said.

Jeremy sat back in his seat. Forgetting that Skippy's head still lay in his lap, he attempted to cross his legs. After a moment, he gave up. "I wasn't close with the guy so I'm not sure how helpful I can be. What did you want to know?"

"I wanted to ask again if you ever heard

any rumors about Dan and other women?" I asked.

Jeremy's eyebrows rose up in surprise. "No, I can't say that I did," he said.

"Really?" I said. "Not one little suggestion that Dan was using his apartment for more than extra work space?"

Jeremy shook his head. "No. Nothing. Dan had a reputation as being an egotistical jackass, but I never heard anything about him cheating."

I nodded. "I see. What about *your* relationship with him?"

Jeremy's brows came together in a practiced expression of confusion. "*My* relationship?" he said slowly. "I'm not sure I understand. We had no relationship." He paused and added, "And in any case, he wasn't my type, if you know what I mean." He tried and failed for a cocky smile.

"I meant, why did you visit his work apartment two days before he died?" I asked.

Jeremy's hand froze mid-stroke over Skippy's head. "I . . . oh that?" he said, attempting a shrug. "Dan wanted to know if I'd be interested in taking the lead in a play he was producing."

I frowned. "Really? From the security video it looks as if you were arguing."

"You saw the security video?" Jeremy

asked, his face going pale.

"Yes," I lied.

Jeremey let out a groan as another voice rang out. "You stupid son-of-a-bitch!" it shouted. "I told you not to go there! Jesus, do you never listen?"

All three of us turned to the source of the voice. It was Jeremy's agent Julie. She was standing on the staircase landing, glaring at Jeremy. She was also dripping wet and wearing only a towel.

Jeremy let out a grown. "Babe," he croaked. "I didn't know you were up."

"Oh, do you want to play the Let's Trade Obvious Statements Game?" Julie sneered, "Fine. You're a complete idiot. Your turn."

Jeremy winced. "Julie, please. It's not what you think."

Julie crossed her arms over her chest. Her gaze slid to mine. "Nic, did I just hear you tell Jeremy that he was captured on the security video at Dan's apartment?"

I nodded. "You did."

Nigel gave a polite wave. "Hi, Julie," he said affably, as if we weren't eavesdropping on a fight between two people, one of whom was wearing only a towel. Later Nigel would claim that his nonchalant reaction was the result of good breeding. I said that it was more likely the result of too many youthful escapades. I would be right.

Julie's gaze shifted back to Jeremy. "Why did you go there, Jeremy? Why? After I specifically told you not to!"

Jeremy swallowed and looked to me as if I had the answer. I didn't. His head swung back to Julie, his eyes panicked. "I . . . I don't know. I don't remember going there," he said. "But . . . I guess . . . I guess I did," Jeremy said, his expression becoming even more morose.

Julie's faced burned red. "You *guess* you did?" she yelled. "What in the actual hell, Jeremy?"

Jeremy lowered his eyes. "I'm sorry, Jules. I really am. I . . . don't remember it, I swear."

Julie exhaled loudly. "Perfect. Just perfect," she sneered. "I'm good, Jeremy, but not that good. If you killed that son-of-a-bitch, then you're on your own. Even I can't help you out of this one."

"Julie, come on," he pleaded. "You'll figure something out. You always do."

Julie let out a strangled cry. "That's it!" she yelled. "I'm done! Do you hear me? Done! Figure your shit out on your own. I'm out!" She turned and ran back up the stairs. Seconds later I heard a door slam.

FORTY

"Shit," Jeremy muttered as he leapt awkwardly off the couch and ran after her. He missed one of the stairs and for a brief moment I thought he was going to end up flat on his face. However, his balance kicked in and he stayed upright. With determination, if not grace, he launched himself up the remaining stairs. Seconds later we heard pounding on a door. "Julie!" Jeremy's panicked voice bellowed. "Julie, honey, please open the door." More pounding ensued. "Dammit, Julie, baby. I'm sorry, okay?" he said, his voice desperate. "I'm really sorry. Please don't leave me, Julie. I love you! I need you. I screwed up. I get that. Please. I'll do anything! Just open the damn door!"

Nigel and I looked at each other at the same time. *"Baby?"* I said.

"I love you?" Nigel said.

My eyes flickered to the stairs where the

pounding had stopped. I glanced back at Nigel. "We were just repeating what Jeremy said, right?" I asked, my voice a whisper.

"What?" Nigel said, affecting confusion. "No. I just thought now seemed the perfect time to express my feelings."

I laughed. "Okay, *baby.*"

There was a sudden commotion as Julie reappeared. Her hair was still wet, but at least she was wearing clothes. She stomped down the stairs with Jeremy in close pursuit. "Julie, please," he whined. "Don't leave me."

"I'm out, Jeremy," she said. "Out. I've had it with your drinking. I've done everything I could to save your sorry ass, but you just don't get it. Figure it out yourself."

Without a backwards glance, she pushed past him and stormed out into the foyer. Seconds later the front door opened and then slammed shut with a reverberating thud. Jeremy's shoulders sagged at the sound.

FORTY-ONE

Jeremy turned and shuffled into the living room. He flopped down into a chair and hung his head in his hands. "I need a drink," he muttered.

"If you mean coffee, then I agree," said Nigel. "If you mean anything stronger, then I'm going to have to tell you that you're delusional."

Jeremy muttered something incoherent and dropped his head even lower. "Coffee, it is," Nigel said cheerfully. Rising from the couch he snapped his fingers. "Come on, Skippy," he said as he headed toward the kitchen, "it's time you learned how to make a decent cup of coffee. You tend to make it too watery." Skippy raised his large head and regarded Nigel for a moment before rising up and trailing after him.

Jeremy's head popped up. He watched Skippy's retreating form and looked over at me. "Your dog makes coffee?" he asked me.

"Not very well, apparently," I answered as I settled back into the couch. "Why don't you tell me about Dan. Why did you go to see him?"

Jeremy shook his head. "But that's just it," he said. "I don't know! I don't remember going there."

"That's not what you told the police."

Jeremy stared at me, his eyes panicked. "I know. I didn't know what to do. I was as surprised as anyone to find out that I'd gone there. I figured that if I told the police that I was blacked out, it would look bad. So I lied."

"But you must have some idea why you went there," I said. "Obviously you had discussed it with Julie."

Jeremy's gaze dropped to the floor. "I suppose I could think of a reason," he said, his voice low. "But I don't know . . ." He looked back up at me. His eyes were red and desperate. "Do you think Julie is going to come back?" he asked me. "I feel like I should talk to her first."

"Why?" I asked.

Jeremy gave a small shrug. "Because she's my wife," he said, looking down at his hands.

"Your wife?" I repeated. "Oh, I see."

Jeremy blinked back up at me. "You do?"

he asked, his voice hopeful.

"No, not really," I admitted.

"Oh," Jeremy said, looking back to his hands. "She's . . . she's been so supportive of me over these last couple of months. I mean, with my announcement and everything. Not a lot of women would stay."

"Well, to be fair, announcing you're gay is kind of a deal breaker for a marriage," I said.

Jeremy let out a sigh. "But that's just the thing," he said. "I'm not gay."

FORTY-TWO

"Pardon?" I said.

Jeremy nodded. "You heard me. I'm not gay."

I frowned. "Don't take this the wrong way," I said, "because — all God's children and all that — but why in the hell would you announce to the world that you're gay when you're not?"

Jeremy closed his eyes and sank back into the chair. "Because I was about to be fired from a play I was in. The director said my drinking was becoming a problem. It would have derailed my career. I would be reduced to working in soap operas. I thought if I could come up with a sympathetic excuse for my behavior, then maybe I could salvage everything. The gay community is always so supportive when someone comes out."

It was several seconds before I could find my voice. I stared at Jeremy with horrified disgust. "I'm sorry," I said after a long minute. "Are you saying that you actually faked being gay so you could excuse your drinking and save your career? Are you serious?"

Nigel walked in with a tray of coffee just in time to hear this. His eyes widened. "Please tell me that I misheard what I heard," he said.

"If you heard that Jeremy here faked being gay so he could abuse the goodwill and support of the gay community," I said, "then unfortunately, you heard correctly."

Nigel turned around with the tray and went back into the kitchen. "Then like hell am I serving you coffee," he muttered.

Jeremy shook his head. "I know. It was a horrible thing to do. Julie was furious with me. But I just didn't know what else to do. I was going to lose everything. I was desperate."

"Did someone change the definition of *desperate* to 'narcissistic asshole'?" I asked. "Because unless they did, I think you have the wrong word."

Nigel came back into the room, sans coffee, and sat down on the couch next to me. He stared at Jeremy as if he were a cockroach crawling across his food. "So did Dan find out about your deplorable little scheme?

Is that why you paid him a visit?" Nigel asked.

Jeremy dug his palms into his eyes. "He found out about it, yes," he said after a minute. "I don't know how, but he did. He told me that unless I invested in his play, he'd out me."

"Yeah, you don't get to use that term anymore," Nigel said.

"Dan basically tried to blackmail you into financing his play," I said. "Did you agree?"

Jeremy didn't answer right away. "I said I'd pay him," he said. "I even wrote out a check. But I found the check in my wallet the day after he was killed. I guess I never gave it to him."

I leaned forward in my seat. "Jeremy, I can't begin to tell you how important this is. You need to remember your visit to Dan. What happened?"

Jeremy jerked his head back, his eyes were wild. "Don't you think I've been trying to do just that? Jesus! I've been racking my brain trying to remember something, but it's no good. It's all a dark fog. I remember banging on his door. I remember being angry. After that I remember throwing up. Here. By myself."

"Julie wasn't here?" I asked.

Jeremy blinked. "Julie?" he repeated.

"Aka, your wife?" I said.

Jeremy went still as he realized the implication. "No. She was here. I misspoke."

I cocked my head and smiled at him. "You said you were here by yourself. Alone. I don't think you can qualify that as misspeaking."

Jeremy's mouth went tight. "Call it what you want. She was here. With me. All night."

"Really?" I asked. "She was here when you were at Dan's? How can you be sure?"

Jeremy glared at me "I'm just sure. That's all."

That made one of us, anyway.

FORTY-THREE

After leaving Jeremy's, Nigel turned to me. "Are you sure you still want to visit Frank and Danny?" he asked.

"I don't see how this day can get any weirder," I said. "Might as well go for broke."

Nigel nodded. "You have a point. Okay. To Little's Vittles it is. Wow. I really thought I would never say that again."

"Well, you know what they say, Mr. Martini: 'never say never.' "

Nigel cocked his head. "I thought it was 'never smoke in bed,' " he said.

"That's a good one, too," I admitted. "Right up there with 'don't bet on horses.' "

Nigel stopped and stared at me. "Now that's just crazy talk," he said.

Frank Little was a small-time loan shark who, until a few years ago, worked solely for his older brother, Danny. The two also owned Little's Vittles, a restaurant of doubtful sanitation that served mainly as a means to launder money. After a "business disagreement with a client" that involved a baseball bat and a lengthy hospital stay for said client landed Danny in prison, Frank went into business with a gentlemen by the name of Fat Saul. Like Danny, Fat Saul was also a loan shark, but on a bigger and more sadistic scale. Around the time Danny was paroled, Fat Saul turned up dead, and Frank took over the business. For his part, Danny took over the management of Little's Vittles, claiming that he was now a legit businessman and provider of quality food. Neither, of course, was true.

Little's Vittles was located on a shabby side street on the Lower East Side. From the outside, it looked like your average hole-in-the-wall restaurant. It was only once you stepped inside that Frank and Danny's unique style and vision became apparent.

To say that the décor was garish would be an understatement. The seating was a mix of red velvet and black pleather. The walls were covered in large, colorful murals, the inspiration for which appeared to be a combination of Michelangelo's panels on the Sistine Chapel ceiling and a healthy dose of acid. Danny was depicted as God, but rather than reaching out to give Adam life, he offered a patron a plate of antipasto. The five Sibyls were now depicted as busty waitresses with extremely tight shorts. God's Creation of the Sun, Moon, and Vegetation now featured Danny directing patrons to their tables.

Nigel took a moment to gaze at all the artwork before blessing himself. "It never gets old, does it?" he said to me with a wistful smile.

A blonde in a tight orange dress and matching lipstick sat at the bar filing her nails. Next to her was a chalkboard on which the daily special was noted as THE ITALIAN SCALLION SUB. Without looking up, she said, "We don't open for lunch for another hour."

"Ah, the hand of Fate is kind," Nigel said.

The blonde raised her head and glanced over at us. Her eyes grew wide and she pointed her emery board at Skippy. "What the hell is that?" she asked.

"This is Skippy," Nigel answered. "The Health Department had to get a little creative after the latest round of budget cuts."

The blonde gazed at Skippy with narrowed eyes. "Are you saying he's a Health Inspector?" she asked.

Nigel let out a low laugh and shook his head. "Of course, not," he said. "That would be absurd." The blonde gave a relieved nod. Nigel continued, lowering his voice, "He's only a Junior Assistant Inspector. He's in a totally different pay grade."

The blonde stared at Skippy for another beat and then said, "Well, either way, you'll have to make an appointment. We're not open for business yet."

"Actually, we were hoping to talk to the owners," I said. "Are either Frank or Danny around?"

The blonde eyed me with suspicion. "Are you with the Health Department, too?" she asked.

"No," I said. "Just an old friend of Danny and Frank's."

The blonde gave me a doubtful once-over. "You don't look like one of their friends," she finally said.

I smiled. "You flatter me. Are they here?"

With a sigh, the blonde slid off her perch at the bar and sashayed back to the kitchen. Pushing the door open, she leaned her head around the corner and yelled, "Danny? There's some people here to see you. I think they might be from the Health Department or something."

A few moments later, Danny appeared.

He was a tall, burly man with thick black hair and an equally thick skull. His wide face was pockmarked; some of the scars were from bad brawls, some merely from bad hygiene. Seeing me, his lips pulled down into a deep scowl. "Jesus, Martini," he grumbled. "Not you again. I thought we were done with your visits."

I placed a hand over my heart. "Danny," I said, "you wound me. Haven't you missed me? Not even a little?"

"What the hell is going on here, Danny?" the blonde asked, her arms now folded across her ample chest. "You screwing around on me? Cause I swear to God, if I find out you are, you're going to be walking funny for a week."

"Shut the hell up, Marie," Danny snapped. "I ain't screwing around with *her,*" he said waving a beefy hand in my direction. "She's an ex-cop, for christsake!"

"You always were a man of high standards, Danny," Nigel said affably. "I admire that."

Danny let out a sigh and leaned against the bar. "What do you want, Martini?" he said.

"I want to know about your business with Dan Trados," I said.

Danny's eyes narrowed. "And why would I tell you that?" he asked.

"Because deep down you want to do the right thing," I said agreeably. "And who knows? You might find it beneficial to help me."

Danny gave me a grim smile. "You threatening me?" he asked.

"No, of course not," I said. "I just need to know about your relationship with Dan Trados."

Danny crossed his arms over his chest and studied me for a beat. "Who says I had a relationship with the guy?" he asked.

I cocked my head. "*Had,* Danny? *Had?* Any reason you're using the past tense?"

Danny blinked. "Look, Martini, I ain't done nothing wrong, and I don't have time to stand around jawing with you. I got a lunch menu to get ready. You got no reason to be hassling me. I run a clean business here."

"Oh Danny," I said. "I have missed your ironic homonyms."

Marie turned on Danny, her eyes flashing with anger. "If you two ain't fooling around," she snarled, "then how the hell does she know about your hommything?"

The door behind me suddenly banged open. I turned around to see Frank Little enter the restaurant. Frank had the same dark hair, thick build, and wide face as his brother, but on a smaller scale. His propensity for violence wasn't as pronounced, either, which was perhaps why he was my favorite of the two brothers.

Frank took one look at me and stopped cold in his tracks. "Shit, Martini," he said. "What are you doing here?"

"Well, sadly, I'm not here for lunch," I said, gesturing to the chalkboard. "That Italian Scallion sub sounds delightful. I'm here because of Dan Trados."

Frank watched me warily. "What about him?" he asked.

"I want to know what your business with him was," I said. "Did he owe you money?"

Frank rolled his eyes at me. "Right, Martini. Like I'm going to discuss my business with you. Why the hell should I tell you anything?"

"Because it'll make you feel good inside to help out an old friend?" I offered with a bright smile.

"We were never friends, Martini," he scoffed.

"Oh Frank, come on," I said. "Don't be like that. Why is your phone number in his phone?"

Frank sighed and pull out a bar stool and sank down onto it. "Get me a whiskey, will ya, Marie?" he said.

Marie nodded and went behind the bar. Pulling down a bottle, she poured some into a glass and shoved it across the bar to Frank. Danny plopped down on a stool next to Frank. "Pour me one, too, Marie," he said.

Marie slammed the bottle down in front of him. "Pour it your damn self, you two-timing bastard," she snarled at him before flouncing off to the kitchen.

Frank watched her go, his expression curious. "What's eating her?" he asked.

Danny shrugged. "She thinks I'm fooling around with Martini."

Frank turned and gaped at his brother. "She thinks you're fooling around with him?" he asked, jerking his thumb in Nigel's direction.

Danny responded by slapping Frank on the back of his head. "Don't be stupid. She thinks I'm fooling around with Nic."

Frank blinked at his brother and then burst out in hysterical laughter. "That's even crazier!" he howled.

Danny glowered at Frank as he poured himself a drink. "Don't know what the hell you think is so funny," he grumbled. "Lots of chicks dig me."

"Not chicks like Nic," Frank said.

"Gentlemen," I said. "As scintillating as

this discussion is, can we get back to the subject of Dan Trados?"

Frank took a sip and looked over at Nigel and me. "Fine. You two want a drink?" he asked.

"No, but thanks," I said. Nigel and I took a seat at the bar. Skippy sat down between us.

Frank glanced down at Skippy. "Swear to God, Martini," he said, "That's the craziest animal I've ever seen. Are you sure it's a dog?"

"Only on his mother's side," I said. "Now tell me why your name is in Dan Trados's contacts. Did he borrow money from you?"

Frank sighed and took another sip. "No, he didn't. He wanted information."

"About what?" I prompted.

"About some guy. What was his name?" he muttered to himself. "You know the one," he said to me. "Chevy Chase."

I blinked at Frank in confusion. "Dan wanted information about Chevy Chase?" I asked.

Frank rolled his eyes and shook his head. "Don't be stupid, Martini. What was that movie he was in? The one when he's the reporter?"

"*Fletch*?" I guessed.

Frank snapped his fingers. "That's the

one. This Dan guy wanted information on Fletcher Irwin."

"Fletcher *Levin,* the producer?" I clarified.

Frank nodded. "That's the guy."

"Well, what did you tell him?" I asked.

Frank took a sip of his drink. "Same thing I'm going to tell you. It's none of your business. I don't discuss my clients."

"Well, I have some news that just might change your mind on that lofty business motto," I said.

Frank looked over at me his eyes wary. "Yeah? What?"

"Dan Trados was found dead two days ago," I said. "He was murdered, to be precise."

"It's good to be precise," Nigel concurred.

Frank slammed down his glass on the wooden bar. "Just what the hell are you getting at, Martini?" he asked. "I ain't got nothing to do with that. You ain't pinning some shitty theater critic's death on me, ya hear?"

I crossed my arms and stared at Frank. "You knew Dan was a theater critic?" I asked.

Frank rolled his eyes. "What? You think you're the only person who likes the theater, Martini? Danny and I like a good play just as much as anyone."

Next to him, Danny poured them each another shot as he nodded his head in agreement. "The man could be real nasty sometimes in his reviews," Danny said. "But he knew good theater."

Frank shrugged. "I didn't like his last review of *Les Mis,* though," he said. "He said Éponine's song 'On My Own' sounded like a screeching cat."

"The man's entitled to his opinion," Danny argued.

"I suppose," sniffed Frank. "I still say he was wrong."

"Well, now he's dead," I said, interrupting. "And I want to know what he was trying to learn about Fletcher Levin."

Frank regarded me with a baleful eye. "Why do you care anyway?" he asked. "You back on the force or something?"

I shook my head. "No. But Dan was married to one of my closest friends," I said. "And I want to help her find his killer."

"How'd he die?" Danny asked me.

"Poison," I replied.

Danny shook his head. "I don't know no one who uses that to off someone."

"Me neither," agreed Frank.

"Well, I suppose everyone has their own particular preference," I said. Both men nodded. "What did Dan want to know about Fletcher? Did he owe you money?"

Frank shot me a baleful look. "The man's walking, ain't he? You think I'd let someone stiff me?"

"Point taken," I said. "Did Fletcher ever borrow money?"

Frank paused and glanced at Danny. Danny gave a faint nod. Frank let out a sigh and said, "Yeah. He did. Borrowed a few grand a few years back. But he paid it back, so we're square."

I thought about this. "But if Fletcher needed to borrow money, why wouldn't he just go to a bank?" I wondered.

Frank laughed. "Not everyone wants to leave a paper trail when they borrow money, Martini."

"When did Dan contact you about this?" I asked.

Frank closed his eyes to think. "A few weeks ago, I guess. He was a real pain in the ass about it, if you want to know the truth. Acted like his shit didn't smell, too. I hate guys like that."

"Did you tell him that Fletcher had borrowed money from you?" I asked.

Frank looked down at his glass. "We may have come to some kind of understanding

about that information," he said after a moment.

I smirked. "Meaning you made him pay
you for the information," I guessed.

"Hey," Frank groused, "I don't show up
at your office and tell you how to run your
business."

"For which I am eternally grateful, Frank,"
I said.

FORTY-FOUR

After talking to Frank, I called Zack, hoping he could shed some light on why Dan was digging around in Fletcher Levin's past. Zack said he could meet at his office that afternoon. An hour later, Nigel, Skippy, and I were ushered into a conference room on the forty-first floor of the World Trade Center. The receptionist, a sleek young woman named Chloe, told us that Zack would be with us momentarily and asked if we'd like any coffee. We told her we did. "But none for Skippy, here," said Nigel. "It keeps him up at night."

Chloe nodded as if this made perfect sense. "I'll be just a moment," she said with a brisk nod. She turned and glided from the room on a pair of Jimmy Choo shoes that probably retailed for more than my first car. Nigel and I took a seat at a long glass table. In front of us, floor-to-ceiling windows looked out at the city below. A minute later,

Zack came into the room. "Hello Mr. and Mrs. Martini," he said as he took a seat at the table. "How can I help you?"

"It seems that Dan was trying to find out something about Fletcher Levin. He borrowed money from a loan shark a few years back, which does seem odd. Do you know what Dan was looking for?"

Zack pushed his glasses up on his nose and leaned his arms on the table. He frowned as he considered the question. "I wonder if it could have had anything to do with that play he was involved in," he said after a few minutes.

"What play?" I asked.

Chloe returned just then with a tray of coffee. She set the tray down and handed Nigel and me our cups. "Thank you, Chloe," Zack said.

"Of course, Mr. Weems," she answered. "Incidentally, the IT guys are here to install the new software you requested. They need your passcode to proceed."

"Oh, sure," said Zack. "It's 62442."

Chloe smiled. "62442," she repeated. "Got it. Thanks."

Chloe left, and I grinned at Zack. "Please tell me you created that code," I said.

Zack looked at me in surprise. "I did," he said with a shy smile. "You're the first person who got it."

Nigel looked at both of us blankly. "What am I missing?" he asked.

"It's the entrance code for the Ministry of Magic in Harry Potter," I said. "If you use a telephone pad, the numbers spell out MAGIC."

Nigel just stared at me. "Of course they do," he said. "How silly of me not to have known that."

I laughed and turned back to Zack. "Don't mind Nigel," I said. "He's a Muggle."

Zack tried to hide his smile as Nigel rolled his eyes. "You were telling us about Fletcher's play?" Nigel prompted.

Zack nodded and pushed his glasses back up again before answering. "A few years ago, Fletcher was asked to invest in a production of Hitchcock's *North-By-Northwest*," he said. "There was a lot of buzz about the play and the rumor was that the big chase scene through the cornfield was going to make the helicopter scene in *Miss Siagon* look primitive. But a production like that needs a lot of money and Fletcher said he knew of some other investors who might be interested in the play. An agreement was eventually reached in which Fletcher would round up the other investors in exchange for a kind of finder's fee."

"Is that standard practice?" Nigel asked.

Zack shrugged. "It's not unheard of. In any case, Fletcher found two overseas investors who agreed to fund the play. However, while Fletcher got his fee, the investors never produced the money. One of them died under rather mysterious circumstances and the other had his assets frozen in some government tax dispute and purportedly fled his country and disappeared. People began to wonder if Fletcher hadn't made up the investors, as he was the only one who ever had any direct contract with them. Dan said he'd found some documents that seemed to indicate that that's exactly what Fletcher had done. That was going to be one of his stories for the book."

I stared at Zack in surprise. "But that doesn't make any sense. Dan wanted Fletcher to invest with him in producing a new play. Why would he risk pissing him off?"

Zack shifted in his seat and gave a non-committal shrug. I slotted this info in with what I already suspected. "Did Dan tell Fletcher that he was going to include that story if Fletcher didn't invest in his play?" I asked. "Could he have been using it as leverage?"

Zack gave a resigned nod. "I don't know

for sure," he said, "but I think he might have."

FORTY-FIVE

Harper's father arranged for bail. After all the red tape was formally dealt with and her bond was posted, she was finally released. Once she was home, Donald called Nigel and me and asked us to come over. I could tell that he was anxious about the police's case against Harper and hoped that I might be able to help. I watched Harper now as she sat on her living room couch snuggling with a sleeping Gracie. Her normally perfectly styled hair was pulled back into a messy ponytail. Her usually tailored clothes were wrinkled and mismatched. Purple smudges stood out against the pale skin under her eyes. But as she gazed down at Gracie, I thought I'd never seen her more content. It was as if Dan's death was forgotten — or no longer mattered. I wasn't sure which was better — or worse — depending on your viewpoint.

"I appreciate your coming over, Nic,"

Donald said as he handed Nigel and I each a glass of scotch. "But the sooner we figure out who really killed Dan, the better this will all be for Harper."

"Of course, Mr. Remington," I said as I glanced back at Harper. She smiled down at Gracie, lightly tracing her finger over her cheek. I couldn't tell if she'd even heard her father's words.

"Have you been able to find out anything so far?" Donald asked.

I took a sip of my drink and nodded. "I have, actually," I said. "But not all of it helps Harper's case, I'm afraid."

Donald sat down heavily in the chair next to mine. His face appeared to have aged ten years over the past few days. "I know Harper didn't kill her husband," he said. "Which means someone else did. Which means there's evidence. We just need to find it."

"I agree with you," I said. "But we need to be able to explain some of Harper's actions. For instance, why did she tell the police that she'd never been to Dan's work apartment, and yet was captured on video doing exactly that?"

Both Donald and I looked over to Harper, who was still absorbed with Gracie. "Harper," Donald said now, his tone gentle,

"Why did you go to Dan's apartment that night?"

Harper slowly tore her gaze away from Gracie. "Hmmm?" she asked.

Donald frowned. "Why did you go to Dan's?" he repeated, his tone less patient.

Harper blinked at her father; her blue eyes unsure. "Because I knew he wasn't there," she said in a small voice. "I was looking for evidence."

"What kind of evidence?" Donald asked.

Harper glanced again at Gracie before answering. "I wanted to know if he was having an affair," she said. "I thought if I found evidence, it would help me in the divorce. So one day I took his key and made a copy of it."

"Did you find anything?" I asked.

Harper shook her head. "No. Nothing. I looked all over that apartment. There wasn't anything there; no condoms, no tea. I searched his desk, too. All that was there was a copy of his manuscript, a copy of that *Yeti* play he was trying to produce, and a query letter from a playwright. There were notes for the manuscript all over his desk. There were notes written in the margins of that play he wanted to produce, too. That's what I don't get. It really seemed like he was working there."

266

"That's interesting," I said.

Donald looked at me sharply. "Why is that?" he asked.

"Because when I got there, there wasn't anything on his desk," I said. "No manuscript, no play, and no query letter. In fact, there were no work-related papers in his apartment at all."

"I don't understand," Donald said. "Are you saying the killer took the manuscript?"

I stared at my glass. "I'm not sure," I said after a minute. "I could see why someone might want to get rid of the book Dan was working on. It sounds as if it was full of stories that might embarrass more than one person. But why would they take the play and a query letter?"

I looked to Harper but she shrugged. "I don't know," she said. "It was just your basic query letter asking Dan to read the play and give feedback."

"Do you remember who it was from?" I asked. "Come on, put that photographic memory to use."

Harper closed her eyes in concentration. "It was a funny name, I remember that," she said. After a minute it came to her. "Lockhart," she said. "It was from a G. Lockhart."

Before I could say anything, there was a

knock on the door. Donald excused himself and went to answer it. We heard male voices in the hallway and then a second later Donald reappeared. Fletcher followed close behind.

Seeing Harper, Fletcher's face relaxed. "Oh my dear girl," he said as he crossed the room to stand next to her. "You poor, poor thing. I was horrified when I heard that you'd been arrested. It's simply absurd! If there is anything you need from me, I hope you will only ask."

Harper looked up at Fletcher and produced a polite if not slightly perplexed smile. "That's very kind of you," she said.

Fletcher took a seat next to her on the couch. "My dear, knowing your mother as I did makes me think of you as part of my own family."

From my peripheral vision, I saw Donald's face blanch in revulsion.

"Oh, well, thank you," Harper said before quickly glancing at her father. Donald stared at Fletcher as if a troll had suddenly sprouted in Harper's living room.

Fletcher now smiled. "I know you must think me presumptuous," he said, "and perhaps I am. But I didn't get to where I am in this life by not stepping forward and speaking my mind. I go after what I want, and right now what I want is to make sure that you don't go to jail."

Harper flinched slightly at his words. The movement startled Gracie, who woke with a jerk and began to cry. Harper snuggled her close and tried to soothe her but to no avail. After a minute, she said, "I think she might be hungry. If you'll excuse me."

Fletcher watched her leave the room with an expression of approval.

"The bond between a mother and her child," he mused. "There's nothing quite like it. One of the rare things on this earth that should be protected and treasured." He suddenly turned to me and asked, "Do you have any children, Mrs. Martini?"

"Does Skippy count?" I asked, nodding my head to where he was sprawled on the floor next to my chair.

Fletcher's gaze moved to where Skippy lay on the floor belly up and paws in the air. It was a position that Nigel had dubbed the Upside-Down Superman. Fletcher offered an indulgent smile. "Not exactly," he said.

I looked over at Skippy. "I'd like to see you try and tell *him* that," I said.

Fletcher laughed. "Well, you are still young," he said. "You still have time. I've always believed that one of life's greatest joys is to have a child," he said.

"So I have heard," I replied diplomatically. I couldn't remember if Fletcher had children of his own and didn't think it polite to ask. I needn't have worried. Fletcher was apparently in a sharing mood. "I never had any children," he said. "Although I wanted to. Very badly, in fact."

"I'm sorry," I said.

Fletcher smiled sadly. "So am I. I came close to settling down a couple of times, but unfortunately, I had to end it. The women I considered marrying had very different ideas of motherhood from myself."

"Oh, I see," I said, when in fact I had no idea what he was talking about.

Fletcher nodded at me as if we understood each other. "I thought you might," he said. "Mothers are meant to stay home with their babies. This new trend of mothers going back to work is appalling. It's why our country is in the mess it's in today. Children need to come home every day to a house that is clean, orderly, and smells of freshly baked cookies."

I began to wonder if Fletcher Levin had recently had a stroke.

"Mothers are the ones who instill their children with a sense of right and wrong," he continued. "They teach them manners and how to act in polite society."

"And what do fathers do exactly?" I asked.

Fletcher stared at me in surprise. "Why, they provide a home and put food on the table," he said. "A man's job is to provide a home. A woman's job is to run it. That's the kind of environment that produces well-adjusted children."

I arched an eyebrow. "I didn't realize there was only one way to raise a child," I said.

Fletcher sniffed. "Well, there is if you want to raise a decent member of society."

Harper returned just then, saving me from making what I'm sure Fletcher would consider a very indecent suggestion. "She's asleep," Harper said as she sat back down on the couch. "Thank God she's too little to understand what's happening."

Fletcher leaned over and took Harper's hand in his. I saw Donald's jaw clench. "My dear," Fletcher said, "what can I do to help? Do you need a lawyer? Money? I'm more than happy to help in any way."

Harper smiled politely and shook her head. "That's very kind of you, Fletcher, but I think I'm fine. My father has retained a lawyer and he's confident in our case."

"Well, you know where to reach me, if you need anything," Fletcher said. "In the meantime, take care of that beautiful baby.

I'll be in touch." He said his good-byes to the rest of us, and Donald walked him to the door. He returned a moment later and sank wearily into a chair.

"Fletcher Levin has got to be the greatest pocket of untapped natural gas known to man," he said.

FORTY-SIX

Later that night, Nigel and I went to the Eugene O'Neill Theater, but this time we went after Peggy's play had ended. I had called Peggy earlier and arranged to meet her backstage. "So why do you want to talk to Brooke?" Peggy asked me when she saw me.

"I just wanted to ask her a few questions about Dan," I said.

Peggy folded her arms over her chest and raised her eyebrow. "Gee, thanks for clearing that up," she said. "I was really confused before, but now it all makes sense."

"Sarcasm isn't attractive on you, Peggy," I said.

"Really? Well, gosh darn it. There goes my day. However, I could say the same thing about you and pig-headed secrecy," she countered.

I laughed. "Peg, I swear I'll tell you everything, but I want to talk to Brooke first."

Peggy uncrossed her arms with a frustrated sigh. "Fine," she said. "She's in her dressing room. It's down the hall on the right."

"Thanks, Peg. I owe you one," I said.

Peggy rolled her eyes. "You really need to learn how to count," she huffed.

"Who is it?" Brooke called out after I'd knocked on her door.

"It's Nic and Nigel Martini," I said. Nigel nudged me and shot me a meaningful look. "And Skippy," I added. Nigel nodded approvingly.

There was a pause and then the sound of movement. A minute later, Brooke called out, "Come on in." I opened the door. Brooke sat at her dressing table, facing the mirror. She wore a peach-colored silk robe that was knotted at the waist. Her blond hair was pulled back into a low ponytail. She was in the process of wiping off her stage makeup. Nigel and I weren't her only company. Mark sat on a small couch to her left. He wore jeans, a blue blazer, and what appeared to be the faint remnants of Brooke's lipstick on his mouth.

"Hello, Mark," I said. "I hope we're not interrupting."

Mark produced an affable smile. "Not at

all," he said. "I was just going over some notes on the play with Brooke." His gaze dropped to Skippy and his mouth dropped open a bit. "Dear God," he said. "Is that a dog?"

Nigel glanced down at Skippy. "Well, that's the rumor, anyway," he said. "His name is Skippy."

Mark tore his gaze from Skippy and glanced up at Nigel, his face incredulous. "Bullshit," he said.

Nigel laughed. "I kid you not." Skippy ambled over to Mark and stuck his nose in his crotch. "I think he likes you," Nigel said as Mark stared down in surprise at Skippy's enormous head.

"Yeah, funny, I got the same impression," Mark said.

Brooke put down her facecloth and turned around to face us. "I'm going to go out on a limb here and guess that you two aren't here to compliment me on my performance tonight," she said with an easy smile.

"Sadly, no," I said. "Although, I'm sure you performed brilliantly."

Brooke raised an eyebrow, silently inviting me to continue.

"I wanted to ask you about Dan Trados," I said.

Brooke picked her facecloth back up and

resumed washing her face. "What about him?"

"Well, I understand that he was writing a book when he died," I said. "Among other things, he was going to include interesting theater anecdotes."

Brooke briefly glanced at me in the mirror before turning her attention back to wiping off her makeup. "Okay," she said in a bored voice.

"Apparently one of his stories was about you."

This time Brooke's gaze stayed on mine. "Oh?" she said. "Is that so?"

Mark sat up straighter on the couch; no small feat considering that Skippy's head was still buried in his lap.

I nodded. "Something about an accident on the set of *Annie*?"

Brooke's eyes narrowed. "What about it?"

I affected a disinterested shrug. "Well, it isn't a very flattering story," I said.

"Nasty, unfounded gossip rarely is," she countered.

"Is that what the story is?" I asked. "Unfounded gossip?"

Brooke undid her ponytail and shook it out. Picking up a hairbrush, she began to brush out her long mane. "I can only assume you are referring to that bitch Sally

Martin and her ridiculous story that I pushed her off a stage. I did no such thing. Sally fell. Plain and simple. She fell, and she then tried to blame me. If someone says otherwise, then they are lying."

"Why would Sally make up such a story?" I asked.

Brooke continued to brush her hair. "Because she knew the director was going to replace her with me. She'd missed a few performances due to a cold or something and I had to take over. I nailed it. The director decided that I should be in the lead when we opened on Broadway. Sally found out about it before they could tell her and she flipped out. She threw herself off that damn stage and tried to make it seem like I pushed her. But I never touched her."

"Evidently Dan had found someone who says you did," I said.

Brooke scoffed. "You mean he found a liar."

"Why would someone lie about that?" I asked.

Brooke slammed her brush down on the table. "How the hell should I know? Maybe they like the notoriety, maybe they have an axe to grind, or maybe somebody bribed them to say it."

"Somebody like Dan?" I asked.

Brooke smirked. "You said it, honey, not me."

I crossed my arms and leaned back against the door. "Why would Dan bribe someone to confirm a story like that?" I asked.

Brooke pulled her hair back up and secured it with a hair tie. "Well, I guess you'd have to ask Dan that, wouldn't you?" She opened her eyes as if suddenly struck by a thought. "Oh, that's right," she said with an insincere smile. "You can't. Pity."

"Oh, I didn't say that *I* didn't know why Dan wanted the story," I said bluffing. "I only wondered if he'd gotten around to telling *you* about it yet."

Brooke's smile vanished. She slowly turned around in her chair.

"Brooke," Mark said in a warning voice.

"Shut up, Mark," Brooke snapped. "Exactly what are you saying, Mrs. Martini?" she asked, her voice low.

"I just wondered if Dan had gotten around to offering you a choice," I said.

Brooke's eyes narrowed. "A choice?" she repeated.

I nodded. "Yes. A choice between having the story published and perhaps . . . doing Dan a favor?" I cocked my head a bit to the right when I said this last bit. I hoped it implied a *come on, we all know what hap-*

pened here attitude rather than the truth, which was a *here goes nothing Hail Mary.*

Brooke glared at me. "Yes, all right, yes," she finally hissed. "Dan wanted me to do some play he'd found, and yes he threatened to publish that damn story about me pushing Sally off the stage if I didn't do it. I told him to go to hell."

"What was Dan's reaction?"

Brooke's glance slid away from mine briefly and landed on Mark. She blinked and looked back at me. "If I remember correctly, he laughed," she said.

"Really? How odd," I said slowly as I pushed myself off the wall. "Well, I appreciate your taking the time to talk to me."

Brooke blinked at me in surprise. "That's it? That's all you wanted to know?"

I smiled. "Well, I do have one more question, if you don't mind."

"What?"

"That night at Fletcher's afterparty, you spilled your drink on Dan."

"Yes, so?" said Brooke.

"Was it deliberate?" I asked.

Brooke let out a small laugh. "Oh, it most certainly was."

"Because he was flirting with you?"

Brooke blinked at me like I was an idiot. "Well, yes. Not only was he flirting with me, but he was doing it right in front of Nina. I mean, talk about arrogance."

"Why would Nina care?" I asked.

"Because they were having an affair, of course."

I sat back in my chair. "Oh? How did you find out about that?" I asked. "I didn't realize that you and Nina were that close."

Brooke rolled her eyes. "You're kidding, right? It was common knowledge. A child of five could have figured it out."

"I see. Well, you've been very helpful," I said sincerely. "I won't take up anymore of your time."

Brooke glanced to Mark before smiling and saying, "Of course. I'm glad I could help."

Nigel and I were quiet when we left Brooke's dressing room. "Well, I finally think I understand everything," I said.

Nigel looked down at me. "You do?" he asked.

"I do."

He looked at me expectantly for a moment. Slowly his eyes narrowed. "You're not going to tell me, are you?" he asked.

I smiled up at him. "You mean you haven't figured it out?"

Nigel made a rude noise. "I hate it when you do that," he huffed.

I laughed and snaked my arm through his. "Don't mope," I said. "I'll tell you everything. And then I need to call Marcy."

Nigel gave a low whistle of approval when I finished telling him my theory. He pulled me into a tight embrace, saying, "Have I ever told you how sexy your brain is?" he said.

"Not recently," I admitted.

"Then let me rectify that," he said with a grin.

Marcy was a little less effusive when I told her my theory some time later, but she finally agreed to my idea. Once she was on board, I had one more call to make. I crossed my fingers and hoped to hell that Peggy would agree.

FORTY-SEVEN

"Nic, you know I love Peggy, but I don't think I'm up for this," Harper said to me the next day as we made our way into Eugene O'Neill Theater. "Besides, I just saw the play. Why can't she just tell us what she changed?"

"Harper, come on," I said. "She tweaked a scene and wants our opinion on whether it works or not. She said that it really changes the play."

"But why us?" Harper asked. "I mean, we're not playwrights."

I rolled my eyes. "Because she trusts us," I said. "She just wants our input."

It was all a lie, of course, but it was imperative that Harper didn't know the real reason we were watching a rehearsal of Peggy's play. I needed to see her honest reaction.

Once we were inside the theater, Peggy ran over to us. Her color was high and she seemed to have trouble staying still. "Are you okay?" I asked, peering at her face.

"Sure, never better," Peggy squeaked before she began to nervously chew on her thumbnail.

"Peggy, for God's sake, calm down," I said, giving her a hard stare. "It's just a rehearsal."

Peggy glared back at me. "Says you. This new scene changes the entire play. I'm still not sure if it works."

"So if it doesn't work, then don't add it," I said.

Peggy chewed her thumbnail again. "It's not as simple as that. Mark called the theater critics and invited them to review the changes. He said that we'd get more publicity that way. For people who haven't seen the play, it might be an inducement for them to see it."

"That makes sense," I said, nodding.

"But what if they hate the changes?" Peggy asked. "What if I ruin everything? I swear to God, if I can get through this rehearsal without developing an ulcer, it'll be a medical miracle."

"Peggy," I soothed, "it'll be fine."

I glanced around the theater. A handful of seats were occupied. I spotted Julie sitting in an aisle seat near the front row. Seeing me, she gave a curt nod and then looked away. Dark purple circles stood out under her eyes. Her complexion was dull and her hair was lank. The past few days had clearly not been easy for her.

Across the aisle from Julie, Zack was hunched down in his seat, making notes on a legal pad. Next to him sat Fletcher. Glancing up, Zack caught my eye and waved. I smiled and waved back. Fletcher noticed his movement and he glanced our way as well. He stood and began to walk toward us. "I'm sure the reviewers will love what you've done," I said to Peggy. "Now, why don't we grab our seats and let you get started." I gave her a hug and whispered, "It'll be fine. You're doing great."

Peggy gave me a tight hug and nodded. "Okay, wish me luck," she said as she hurried backstage.

I glanced over at Harper. "Are you okay?" I asked.

Harper nodded. "I'm just tired, I guess," she said.

"Well, why don't we find a seat then," I said just as Fletcher joined our group.

"My dear girl," he said looking down at Harper. "What on earth are you doing here?"

Harper managed a small smile. "I'm here

284

to support Peggy," she said. "She's a bit nervous about her changes."

Fletcher reached out and gently took her by the arm. "You look exhausted. You really should be home resting," he said. Shooting me an annoyed look, he added, "I would have thought your friends would have better sense than to drag you out for something as inconsequential as this. And where is your daughter?" he asked.

"She's at home with my nanny," Harper said. "But I'm fine. Really, I am," she said. "Besides, I want to be here for Peggy."

Fletcher gave her a dubious look and then led her over to where he was sitting. Nigel and I trailed behind them. As we approached, Julie looked down at her phone and pretended not to see us. Zack, however, immediately stood up. "Hello, Mrs. Trados," he said to Harper, his expression sincere. "It's nice to see you again. How are you doing?"

Harper managed a small smile. "I'm fine, Zack. Thank you for asking. I got your card, by the way. Thank you. It was lovely."

Zack ducked his head in embarrassment. "It was the least I could do," he said.

"Come on, my dear," Fletcher said as he led Harper past Zack and down the aisle a few seats. "Let's get you seated."

"Thank you, Fletcher," Harper said. Nigel and I followed after them. We had just taken our seats when Peggy walked out onto the stage. "I want to thank everyone for coming to our performance this afternoon," she said. "As you all know, I've made some changes to my play. I think they allow me to better illustrate some of the themes I was trying to convey — particularly how family loyalty can be a blessing and a curse." Peggy paused and glanced at me. "Ok, then. Without further ado, here is *Dealer's Choice.*"

The theater lights dimmed and Peggy quickly walked off the stage. I said a fervent prayer that my gamble would pay off.

Forty-Eight

Peggy's new scene was at the end of Act II. Jeremy, Nina, and Brooke were all on stage, in their roles as the struggling Davis family. Brooke's character, Lilly, has just confronted Jeremy's character about his affair with a woman from their town. Jeremy sits at the family kitchen table, with his head in his hands. In front of him is a bottle of what appears to be whiskey. Nina stands at the sink. A plate that she had been washing falls to the floor and smashes. No one moves. "This ends now!" Brooke suddenly yells as she storms out of the room. The stage goes dark. A moment later, it is lit up again. The scene has changed. The kitchen is now empty. The bottle of whiskey sits on the table. A dark figure enters and pours a vial of something into the bottle and leaves. The stage goes dark once more. When the lights come back on, we see that Jeremy is sitting alone in the kitchen. There are papers on the table in front of him. A cot has been moved into the room, implying that he has been kicked out of his bedroom. Jeremy pours himself a large glass of whiskey and drinks it. Seconds later, he begins to cough. He claws at his throat and then finally collapses onto the table. Moments later the dark figure returns to the room. The figure picks up the bottle of whiskey and dumps it down the sink. The figure then pulls a new bottle out of a bag and pours half of it down the drain as well, before setting the bottle down on the kitchen table. The figure washes out the glass that Jeremy used before taking down a second glass from the cupboard. Bringing the rim to its mouth, the figure leaves an imprint of lipstick on the glass. The figure then places both glasses in the sink. Turning back to Jeremy's still form, the figure drags Jeremy to his cot and places him on it. The figure takes the papers from the table and starts to leave.

Next to me, Harper gasped and put her hand over her mouth, just as the theater lights came on. Around me, people blinked in confusion. Peggy suddenly walked out on the stage and stood next to the dark figure. A black ski mask still hid the face of the individual. Peggy reached over and yanked off the mask to reveal Nigel.

"Ladies and gentlemen," she said as she took a deep breath, "please forgive the interruption, but I thought it was important to explain the significance of the scene you just witnessed. You see, what you saw was a reenactment of how Dan Trados was killed."

FORTY-NINE

Fletcher leapt from his seat. "What the hell is going on?" he bellowed. He glanced over at Harper's pale face. "This is outrageous!"

Peggy took a startled step backwards and looked at me. I nodded at her and stood up. "Actually, this was my idea," I said as I made my way up to the stage to stand next to Nigel. "Could the rest of the cast come out on stage now, please?" I asked. "Oh, and you, too, Mark," I added. My phone buzzed with an incoming text. I glanced down and gave a sigh of relief as I read the message from Marcy.

There was an awkward silence as Nina, Brooke, Mark, and Jeremy shuffled out onto the stage. They stared at Peggy in confusion. "Would someone please explain to me the meaning of this?" Nina asked.

"I'd be happy to," I said. "As you all know, Dan Trados was murdered and the police have unfortunately focused their attention on his wife, Harper. I'm here today to prove her innocence."

Brooke glanced nervously at Nina and back at me. "How do you propose to do that?" she asked warily. Mark stepped next to her and grabbed her hand. She leaned back into him.

I smiled at her. "Simple. I know you were told that Peggy had added a new scene to the play, but that's not entirely true," I said.

"Actually, it's not true *at all,*" Nigel said.

I nodded in agreement. "That's true," I admitted. "The scene you just watched was one that *I* wrote. I asked Peggy to pretend that she wanted to add it to the play."

"But why?" Jeremy asked.

"Because I wanted to know what someone's reaction would be," I said. "I didn't mention this part earlier, but everyone was secretly filmed during that scene. It was very illuminating."

"So . . . so you know who killed Dan?" Harper said in a dazed voice from her seat.

I looked over at her and nodded. "Yes, I do." I shifted my gaze to the one pair of eyes; eyes which now held an expression of fear.

"Who?" she asked, her voice barely a whisper.

"Zack Weems," I answered.

FIFTY

Zack blinked at me. "You're kidding, right?" he asked, his voice incredulous. "This has got to be a joke! Why on earth would I kill Dan?"

I walked over to Nigel and took the papers he'd used for the scene out of his hands. "Because of this," I answered.

"Is that Dan's missing manuscript?" Harper asked.

I shook my head. "No, it's *Year of the Yeti,* the play that Dan was trying to get backing for."

Zack shook his head in confusion. "But that makes no sense. Why would I kill Dan over a play?"

"Because *you* wrote that play," I said. "You wrote it and sent it to Dan under an assumed name hoping to get some honest feedback. Instead, Dan wrote back that he didn't like it. But he did. He liked it a lot. In fact, he liked it so much that he stole it.

He changed parts of it, including the name of the playwright. If you'll remember, Dan told everyone that a man named Robert Taylor wrote the play. But that wasn't true. Harper went to Dan's apartment the night before he died and she saw a copy of the play on Dan's desk. The name on the play was G. Lockhart."

Zack looked around the quiet theater and laughed. "So? What does that prove? If you haven't noticed, my name isn't Robert Taylor or G. Lockhart."

I smiled. "Yes. I know. Gilderoy Lockhart is a character from Harry Potter. A character by the way, who wrote a book called *Year with the Yeti*. You're not the only Harry Potter fan, Zack."

Zack opened his mouth but nothing came out. He shook his head. "I'm sorry, but you're grasping at straws here. Just because I like Harry Potter doesn't prove anything," he said.

I tipped my head in acknowledgment. "Not by itself, no. But then I began to think about all the evidence. Dan's apartment was staged to look as if he'd been having an affair. It was well stocked with tea — a drink that Dan hated. There were condoms in the bedroom. Unfortunately, Dan had a latex allergy, so it was doubtful that they were

293

his. In the sink there were two wineglasses, one with a lipstick stain on the rim." I walked over toward the table on the stage. "And there was the little problem with the decanter of scotch in Dan's apartment."

Zack blinked. "I don't understand. There wasn't any poison in that decanter," he said.

I gave a slow smile. "I know. However, I don't believe I ever mentioned that to anyone. No, the problem with that decanter wasn't that it had been tampered with. The problem was that it was filled with an inferior variety of scotch. It was Nigel who noticed it, actually." I turned to Nigel with a nod. "An appreciation of fine scotch was one of the few things Nigel had in common with Dan. And then I remembered how at Fletcher's party, you couldn't tell the difference between scotch and whiskey. I began to wonder if you had poisoned Dan's scotch and then later replaced it. It would be so simple to do, really," I said. "You were going over to Dan's apartment all the time anyway to work on the manuscript. You poisoned the scotch and then when Dan was dead, you let yourself back into the apartment and staged it to look like Dan was having an affair."

"But he was having an affair," Zack protested. Pointing at Nina he said, "She admitted it!"

Everyone turned to look at Nina. "Except she wasn't having an affair with Dan," I said. "She only pretended to, to hide the real reason she'd paid a visit to Dan. He was trying to blackmail her."

Nina nodded. "I am so sorry, Harper," she said. "I know my lie must have hurt you terribly."

"You see, when Nina heard that it appeared that Dan was having an affair, she used it to cover the real reason she'd gone to see him," I said.

Fletcher's eyes narrowed. "Which was what?" he asked me.

Nina's startled gaze flew to mine. I saw a silent plea for silence in her blue eyes. I saw a similar expression in Brooke's very similar colored eyes. I looked back at Fletcher and shook my head. "That's not for me to say," I said. "But it had nothing to do with Dan's murder." Nina let out a sigh of relief. "I was struck from the beginning that while most people disliked Dan, no one thought he was the kind of man to cheat on his wife."

Harper's head dropped to her chest, and she let out a small sob. Fletcher wrapped a comforting arm around her shoulders.

"In fact, the only one to push that narrative was you, Zack," I went on. "You claimed that you hadn't been working late with Dan and hinted that Dan had been using you as an alibi. But Dan *was* working late with you. You're on the security footage going to his apartment."

Zack stood up and sneered at me. "This is all a very pretty story," he said. "Maybe you can help your friend write her next play. But as for evidence, you don't have a damn thing. Just because I'm a Harry Potter fan doesn't mean I wrote that play. You have no proof."

I shook my head. "Actually, Zack. That's where you're wrong. It's because you are a Harry Potter fan that I was able to get proof. When I visited you in your office a few days ago, you told your secretary your computer password. Remember? It was 62442, the same password Harry uses to get into the Ministry of Magic."

Zack's face paled as he listened.

"So I had my old partner get a warrant to look at your computer. Which she did, while you sat here and watched this little drama unfold. It's all on your computer, Zack. Your play. The letter to Dan. All of it. Isn't that right, Marcy?"

Marcy stepped up behind Zack. Brian stood next to her. "It sure is," Marcy said with a satisfied smile. Zack whirled around and tried to run, but slammed into Brian's chest instead. A moment later, Marcy slapped the cuffs on Zack.

I moved to stand next to Nigel as Marcy began to read Zack his rights. "I think that's the part of being a detective I miss most," I said to Nigel as Marcy led Zack away.

"Reading someone their Miranda Rights?" Nigel asked.

"No. Slapping the cuffs on the suspect," I admitted.

Nigel wrapped his arm around my shoulder. "Well, I'd be happy to play cops and robbers with you later, if it'll make you feel better."

I tucked my head in under his neck. "You sure know how to sweet talk a girl, Mr. Martini," I said.

Nigel kissed the top of my head. "Well, duh," he said.

FIFTY-ONE

An hour later, we were at Harper's apartment. Peggy and Evan sat on the couch. Nigel and I sat across from them in matching club chairs. Harper was in the nursery with Devin trying to put Gracie down for a nap. Donald was busy making us all drinks.

"I still can't wrap my head around all of this," Peggy said. "Dan actually tried to steal his own co-worker's play. What a son-of-a-bitch."

"Quite literally in this case," Donald said dryly as he handed Peggy her drink.

"I guess I owe you an apology for all those times I teased you about being a Harry Potter fanatic," Peggy said, after thanking Donald. "If it hadn't been for your rather, ahem, obsessive knowledge of the books, Zack might have gotten away with it."

I raised my eyebrow. "So much for your apology," I said. Donald handed me my drink and I took a grateful sip.

Harper came down the hallway and flopped onto the couch next to Peggy. "Do you want a drink, honey?" Donald asked.

"God, yes," Harper said.

"Is Gracie asleep?" Peggy asked.

Harper shook her head. "Not quite. She's close though. Devin has her."

"So what's the deal with you two, anyway?" she asked. "Are you going to start seeing him?"

Harper accepted a drink from her father, took a sip, and then leaned her head back against the cushions. "I don't know," she said, closing her eyes. "I know my marriage to Dan was over. But it feels wrong to start anything now. I mean, we just buried him."

Peggy reached over and squeezed Harper's hand. "I know, honey. But that shouldn't stop you from being happy. And I have a feeling that Devin will make you happy. And, if it doesn't work out, send him my way, because he is gorgeous!" she said with a giggle.

Evan rolled his eyes. "You know, that's not nearly as funny as you think it is," he groused.

Peggy laughed and leaned over to kiss his cheek. "Oh, it's a little funny," she said. "Besides, you know I adore you."

Donald handed Evan and Nigel their

drinks and then sat down with us. "So Dan not only stole someone's play, but he was also trying to blackmail people into funding it?" he asked me.

I nodded. "He found out that Fletcher had once bilked investors out of thousands of dollars, Brooke was rumored to have pushed a rival off a stage, and that Jeremy was only pretending to be gay to take advantage of the goodwill of the LGBT community."

Harper sneered in disgust. "I still can't believe Jeremy did that. I don't know which is worse, actually. What he did or what Dan did."

"Both are pretty despicable," I said.

"But what did Dan find out about Nina?" Harper asked.

I looked at her in surprise. "I would have thought you'd have figured that out," I said. "Remember, you're the one who told me that Dan had mentioned that Nina had a baby."

Harper opened her eyes wide. "I don't understand," she said. "Why was that so terrible? So what if she had a baby and put it up for adoption? Why would anyone care about that?"

"Well, for one, I think Fletcher Levin

would care a great deal. After all, it was his baby."

Harper's mouth fell open. "Fletcher's baby?" she repeated.

I nodded. "I thought it was odd that after breaking off her engagement with Fletcher, Nina basically went on a one-year hiatus. Especially since she claimed that the whole reason for ending things with Fletcher was because she wanted to focus on her career."

Peggy frowned. "But if Nina and Fletcher were already engaged, why would she give up their baby?"

"It didn't click with me until the day that Fletcher came here to see Harper," I said. "He went on and on about how a woman is meant to stay home with their children. It became clear that he would have forced Nina to abandon her dreams of being an actress."

"So instead she put her baby up for adoption?" Harper asked horrified.

"Well, I don't think she saw the alternative as an option," I said. "When I first met Nina, she made a joke about the nuns who taught her. If she were Catholic, she might not be comfortable terminating a pregnancy."

"But still," said Peggy. "What could Fletcher do to her after all these years?

301

Granted, he could make her life a little difficult, but she's a star in her own right."

I nodded. "Actually, I don't think that Nina was worried about herself. I think she was worried about her daughter."

"Daughter?" Peggy asked.

I nodded again. "Brooke Casey is Nina and Fletcher's daughter."

"Get the hell out!" Peggy said. "How the hell did you figure that out?"

I smiled. "Well, Zack mentioned to me how Brooke was adopted. And then there was the fact that Brooke intentionally dumped her wine on Dan at Fletcher's party. After she did, I saw her wink at Nina. When I asked her about the wink, she said it was because Dan was flirting with her in front of Nina. She claimed it was a form of retaliation because she knew that Nina and Dan were having an affair."

Peggy frowned at me. "But you said that Dan and Nina weren't having an affair."

"They weren't," I said. "And everyone I talked to seemed surprised at the idea that Dan would cheat on Harper. The only ones who said otherwise were Zack, Nina, and Brooke. Brooke actually made it a point to tell me that Dan was a well-known philanderer and that it was widely known that he and Nina were having an affair." I paused

302

and then said, "I thought it odd that two women with supposedly no connection other than a play would tell the same lie."

Peggy stared at me a beat and then said, "You know what, Nic? I love you to death, but sometimes your brain scares the shit out of me. Remind me never to cross you."

FIFTY-TWO

When Nigel and I returned to our hotel room, we found that an enormous bouquet of flowers had been delivered. Attached was a note addressed to me. Nigel went to make us two dirty martinis while I read the note. It was from Nina. *Dear Nic,* it read, *Thank you from the bottom of my heart for your discretion. Tell Nigel he's a lucky man. Much love, Nina.*

"Who are the flowers from?" Nigel asked as he mixed our drinks.

"Nina," I said. "She thanked me for not telling Fletcher about Brooke and to tell you that you're a lucky man."

Nigel laughed. "That, my dear, is what they call 'burying the lede.' "

"I wasn't aware that you were so well versed in publishing," I said.

"I spent a summer interning for *The Times,*" he said as he handed me my martini. "I learned quite a bit actually."

"Really," I said with a smile. "About burying the lede?"

Nigel winked. "Among other things. If you're nice, I'll explain what 'below the fold' means."

"Sounds quite titillating," I said as I took a sip of my drink.

"How's your martini, by the way?" Nigel asked. "Dirty enough for you?"

I smiled. "Never."

RECIPES

THE LEADING MAN
Ingredients:
2 oz. whiskey
0.5 oz. sweet vermouth
1 dash bitters (optional)
1 cup ice cubes
1 maraschino cherry for garnish

Preparation:
Place ice in a mixing glass. Pour in vermouth, then whiskey, and stir. Strain into a cocktail glass. Add a dash of bitters if desired, and garnish with a cherry.

THE CURTAIN CALL
Ingredients:
3 oz. bourbon
1.5 oz. vermouth
6 dashes bitters

Preparation:
Add all the ingredients to a large glass filled with ice and stir.

THE UNDERSTUDY

Ingredients:
2 oz. tequila
1 oz. sweet vermouth
2 dashes orange bitters

Preparation:
Add all the ingredients to a mixing glass and fill with ice. Stir, and strain into a chilled cocktail glass. Garnish with a lime twist or a cherry.

THE STAGE RIGHT

Ingredients:
1.5 oz. rye whiskey
0.5 oz. sweet vermouth
0.5 oz. Cardamaro
4 dashes bitters
1 maraschino cherry for garnish

Preparation:
Combine rye, vermouth, Cardamaro, and bitters in a cocktail shaker filled with ice. Shake and strain into a chilled martini glass; garnish with cherry.

ABOUT THE AUTHOR

Tracy Kiely received a BA in English from Trinity College. This accomplishment prompted most job interviewers to ask, "How fast can you type?" Her standard answer of "not so fast" usually put an end to further questions.

She was eventually hired by the American Urological Association (AUA), who were kind enough to overlook the whole typing thing — mainly because they knew just what kind of prose she'd be typing. After several years, Tracy left the AUA, taking with her a trove of anecdotal stories that could eventually result in her banishment from polite society. That's when she thought writing a novel might be a good idea.

Murder with a Twist was her first novel in the Nic & Nigel Martini series. It can be enjoyed straight up or with a twist. She is also the author of the Jane Austen–inspired Elizabeth Parker mystery series: *Murder at*

Longbourn, Murder on the Bride's Side, Murder Most Persuasive, and *Murder Most Austen.* These can be enjoyed with either tea or a very dry sherry.

Tracy lives in Maryland with her husband and three children.

The employees of Thorndike Press hope you have enjoyed this Large Print book. All our Thorndike, Wheeler, and Kennebec Large Print titles are designed for easy reading, and all our books are made to last. Other Thorndike Press Large Print books are available at your library, through selected bookstores, or directly from us.

For information about titles, please call:
  (800) 223-1244

or visit our website at:
  gale.com/thorndike

To share your comments, please write:
  Publisher
  Thorndike Press
  10 Water St., Suite 310
  Waterville, ME 04901